THE BODY HUMAN

THE BODY HUMAN

THREE STORIES OF FUTURE MEDICINE

NANCY KRESS

an imprint of

ARC
MANOR
Rockville, Maryland

ISBN: 978-1-61242-065-3

www.PhoenixPick.com
Great Science Fiction & Fantasy
Free Ebook every month

"Evolution" by Nancy Kress. Copyright © 1995 by Nancy Kress. First published in *Asimov's Science Fiction*, October 1995.

"Fault Lines" by Nancy Kress. Copyright © 1995 by Nancy Kress. First published in *Asimov's Science Fiction*, August 1995.

"The Mountain to Mohammed" by Nancy Kress. Copyright © 1992 by Nancy Kress. First published in *Isaac Asimov's Science Fiction Magazine*, April 1992.

Published by Phoenix Pick
an imprint of Arc Manor
P. O. Box 10339
Rockville, MD 20849-0339
www.ArcManor.com

Contents

EVOLUTION

"SOMEBODY SHOT AND KILLED Dr. Bennett behind the Food Mart on April Street!" Ceci Moore says breathlessly as I take the washing off the line.

I stand with a pair of Jack's boxer shorts in my hand and stare at her. I don't like Ceci. Her smirking pushiness, her need to shove her scrawny body into the middle of every situation, even ones she'd be better off leaving alone. She's been that way since high school. But we're neighbors; we're stuck with each other. Dr. Bennett delivered both Sean and Jackie. Slowly I fold the boxer shorts and lay them in my clothesbasket.

"Well, Betty, aren't you even going to *say* anything?"

"Have the police arrested anybody?"

"Janie Brunelli says there's no suspects." Tom Brunelli is one of Emerton's police officers, all five of them. He has trouble keeping his mouth shut. "Honestly, Betty, you look like there's a murder in this town every day!"

"Was it in the parking lot?" I'm in that parking lot behind the Food Mart every week. It's unpaved, just hard-packed rocky dirt sloping down to a low concrete wall by the river. I take Jackie's sheets off the line. Belle, Ariel, and Princess Jasmine all smile through fields of flowers.

"Yes, in the parking lot," Ceci says. "Near the dumpsters. There must have been a silencer on the rifle, nobody heard anything. Tom found two .22 250 semi-automatic cartridges." Ceci knows about guns. Her house is full of them. "Betty, why don't you put all this wash in your dryer and save yourself the trouble of hanging it all out?"

"I like the way it smells line-dried. And I can hear Jackie through the window."

Instantly Ceci's face changes. "Jackie's home from school? Why?"

"She has a cold."

"Are you sure it's just a cold?"

"I'm sure." I take the clothespins off Sean's t-shirt. The front says SEE DICK DRINK. SEE DICK DRIVE. SEE DICK DIE. "Ceci, Jackie is not on any antibiotics."

"Good thing," Ceci says, and for a moment she studies her fingernails, very casual. "They say Dr. Bennett prescribed endozine again last week. For the youngest Nordstrum boy. *Without* sending him to the hospital."

I don't answer. The back of Sean's t-shirt says DON'T BE A DICK. Irritated by my silence, Ceci says, "I don't see how you can let your son wear that obscene clothing!"

"It's his choice. Besides, Ceci, it's a health message. About not drinking and driving. Aren't you the one that thinks strong health messages are a good thing?"

Our eyes lock. The silence lengthens. Finally Ceci says, "Well, haven't *we* gotten serious all of a sudden."

I say, "Murder is serious."

"Yes. I'm sure the cops will catch whoever did it. Probably one of those scum that hang around the Rainbow Bar."

"Dr. Bennett wasn't the type to hang around with scum."

"Oh, I don't mean he *knew* them. Some low-life probably killed him for his wallet." She looks straight into my eyes. "I can't think of any other motive. Can you?"

I look east, toward the river. On the other side, just visible over the tops of houses on its little hill, rise the three stories of Emerton Soldiers and Sailors Memorial Hospital.

The bridge over the river was blown up three weeks ago. No injuries, no suspects. Now anybody who wants to go to the hospital has to drive ten miles up West River Road and cross at the interstate. Jack told me that the Department of Transportation says two years to get a new bridge built.

I say, "Dr. Bennett was a good doctor. And a good man."

"Well, did anybody say he wasn't? Really, Betty, you should use your dryer and save yourself all that bending and stooping. Bad for the back. We're not getting any younger. Ta-ta." She waves her right hand, just a waggle of fingers, and walks off. Her nails, I notice, are painted the delicate fragile pinky white of freshly unscabbed skin.

"You have no proof," Jack says. "Just some wild suspicions."

He has his stubborn face on. He sits with his Michelob at the kitchen table, dog-tired from his factory shift plus three hours overtime, and he doesn't want to hear this. I don't blame him. I don't want to be saying it. In the living room Jackie plays Nintendo frantically, trying to cram in as many electronic explosions as she can before her father claims the TV for Monday night football. Sean has already gone out with his friends, before his stepfather got home.

I sit down across from Jack, a fresh mug of coffee cradled between my palms. For warmth. "I know I don't have any proof, Jack. I'm not some detective."

"So let the cops handle it. It's their business, not ours. You stay out of it."

"I am out of it. You know that." Jack nods. We don't mix with cops, don't serve on any town committees, don't even listen to the news much. We don't get involved with what doesn't concern us. Jack never did. I add, "I'm just telling you what I think. I can do that, can't I?" and hear my voice stuck someplace between pleading and anger.

Jack hears it, too. He scowls, stands with his beer, puts his hand gently on my shoulder. "Sure, Bets. You can say whatever you want to me. But nobody else, you hear? I don't want no trouble, especially to you and the kids. This ain't our problem. Just be grateful *we're* all healthy, knock on wood."

He smiles and goes into the living room. Jackie switches off the Nintendo without being yelled at; she's good that way. I look out the kitchen window, but it's too dark to see anything but my own reflection, and anyway the window faces north, not east.

I haven't crossed the river since Jackie was born at Emerton Memorial, seven years ago. And then I was in the hospital less than twenty-four hours before I made Jack take me home. Not because of the infections, of course—that hadn't all started yet. But it has now, and what if next time instead of the youngest Nordstrum boy, it's Jackie who needs endozine? Or Sean?

Once you've been to Emerton Memorial, nobody but your family will go near you. And sometimes not even them. When Mrs. Weimer came home from surgery, her daughter-in-law put her in that back upstairs room and left her food on disposable trays in the doorway and put in a chemical toilet. Didn't even help the old lady crawl out of bed to use it. For a whole month it went on like that—surgical masks, gloves, paper gowns—until Rosie Weimer was positive Mrs. Weimer hadn't picked up any mutated drug-resistant bacteria in Emerton Memorial. And Hal Weimer didn't say a word against his wife.

"People are scared, but they'll do the right thing," Jack said, the only other time I tried to talk to him about it. Jack isn't much for talking. And so I don't. I owe him that.

But in the city—in all the cities—they're not just scared. They're terrified. Even without listening to the news I hear about the riots and the special government police and half the population sick with the new germs that only endozine cures—sometimes. I don't see how they're going to have much energy for one murdered small-town doctor. And I don't share Jack's conviction that people in Emerton will automatically do the right thing. I remember all too well that sometimes they don't. How come Jack doesn't remember, too?

But he's right about one thing: I don't owe this town anything.

I stack the supper dishes in the sink and get Jackie started on her homework.

The next day, I drive down to the Food Mart parking lot.

There isn't much to see. It rained last night. Next to the dumpster lie a wadded-up surgical glove and a piece of yellow tape like the police use around a crime scene. Also some of those little black cardboard boxes from the stuff that gets used up by the new holographic TV cameras. That's it.

"You heard what happened to Dr. Bennett," I say to Sean at dinner. Jack's working again. Jackie sits playing with the Barbie doll she doesn't know I know she has on her lap. Sean looks at me sideways, under the heavy fringe of his dark bangs, and I can't read his expression. "He was killed for giving out too many antibiotics."

Jackie looks up. "Who killed the doctor?"

"The bastards that think they run this town," Sean says. He flicks the hair out of his eyes. His face is ashy gray. "Fucking vigilantes'll get us all."

"That's enough, Sean," I say.

Jackie's lip trembles. "Who'll get us all? Mommy…"

"Nobody's getting anybody," I say. "Sean, stop it. You're scaring her."

"Well, she should be scared," Sean says, but he shuts up and stares bleakly at his plate. Sixteen now, I've had him for sixteen years. Watching him, his thick dark hair and sulky mouth, I think that it's a sin to have a favorite child. And that I can't help it, and that I would, God forgive me, sacrifice both Jackie and Jack for this boy.

"I want you to clean the garage tonight, Sean. You promised Jack three days ago now."

"Tomorrow. Tonight I have to go out."

Jackie says, "Why should I be scared?"

"Tonight," I say.

Sean looks at me with teenage desperation. His eyes are very blue. "Not tonight. I have to go out."

Jackie says, "Why should I—"

I say, "You're staying home and cleaning the garage."

"No." He glares at me, and then breaks. He has his father's looks, but he's not really like his father. There are even tears in the corners of his eyes. "I'll do it tomorrow, Mom, I promise. Right after school. But tonight I have to go out."

"Where?"

"Just out."

Jackie says, "Why should I be scared? Scared of what? Mommy!"

Sean turns to her. "You shouldn't be scared, Jack-o-lantern. Everything's going to be all right. One way or another."

I listen to the tone of his voice and suddenly fear shoots through me, piercing as childbirth. I say, "Jackie, you can play Nintendo now. I'll clear the table."

Her face brightens. She skips into the living room and I look at my son. "What does that mean? 'One way or another'? Sean, what's going on?"

"Nothing," he says, and then despite his ashy color he looks me straight in the eyes, and smiles tenderly, and for the first time—the very first time—I see his resemblance to his father. He can lie to me with tenderness.

Two days later, just after I return from the Food Mart, they contact me.

The murder was on the news for two nights, and then disappeared. Over the parking lot is scattered more TV-camera litter. There's also a wine bottle buried halfway into the hard ground, with a bouquet of yellow roses in it. Nearby is an empty basket, the kind that comes filled with expensive dried flowers at Blossoms by Bonnie, weighted down with stones. Staring at it, I remember that Bonnie Widelstein went out of business a few months ago. A drug-resistant abscess, and after she got out of Emerton Memorial, nobody on this side of the river would buy flowers from her.

At home, Sylvia James is sitting in my driveway in her black Algol. As soon as I see her, I put it together.

"Sylvia," I say tonelessly.

She climbs out of the sports car and smiles a social smile. "Elizabeth! How good to see you!" I don't answer. She hasn't seen me in seventeen years. She's carrying a cheese kuchen, like some sort of key into my house. She's still blonde, still slim, still well dressed. Her lipstick is bright red, which is what her face should be.

I let her in anyway, my heart making slow hard thuds in my chest. *Sean. Sean.*

Once inside, her hard smile fades and she has the grace to look embarrassed. "Elizabeth—"

"Betty," I say. "I go by Betty now."

"Betty. First off, I want to apologize for not being…for not standing by you in that mess. I know it was so long ago, but even so, I—I wasn't a very good friend." She hesitates. "I was frightened by it all."

I want to say, *You* were frightened? But I don't.

I never think of the whole dumb story anymore. Not even when I look at Sean. Especially not when I look at Sean.

Seventeen years ago, when Sylvia and I were seniors in high school, we were best friends. Neither of us had a sister, so we made each other into that, even though her family wasn't crazy about their precious daughter hanging around with someone like me. The Goddards live on the other side of the river. Sylvia ignored them, and I ignored the drunken warnings of my aunt, the closest thing I had to a family. The differences didn't matter. We were Sylvia-and-Elizabeth, the two prettiest and boldest girls in the senior class who had an academic future.

And then, suddenly, I didn't. At Elizabeth's house I met Randolf Satler, young resident in her father's unit at the hospital. And I got pregnant, and Randy dumped me, and I refused a paternity test because if he didn't want me and the baby I had too much pride to force myself on any man. That's what I told everyone, including myself. I was eighteen years old. I didn't know what a common story mine was, or what a dreary one. I thought I was the only one in the whole wide world who had ever felt this bad.

So after Sean was born at Emerton Memorial and Randy got engaged the day I moved my baby "home" to my dying aunt's, I bought a Smith & Wesson revolver in the city and shot out the windows of Randy's supposedly empty house across the river. I hit the gardener, who was helping himself to the Satler liquor cabinet in the living room. The judge gave me seven-and-a-half to ten, and I served five, and that only because my lawyer pleaded post-partum depression. The gardener recovered and retired to Miami, and Dr. Satler went on to become Chief of Medicine at Emerton Memorial and a lot of other important things in the city, and Sylvia never visited me once in Bedford Hills Correctional Facility. Nobody did, except Jack. Who, when Sylvia-and-Elizabeth were strutting their stuff at Emerton High, had already dropped out and was bagging groceries at the Food Mart. After I got out of Bedford, the only reason the foster-care people would give me Sean back was because Jack married me.

We live in Emerton, but not of it.

Sylvia puts her kuchen on the kitchen table and sits down without being asked. I can see she's done with apologizing. She's still smart enough to know there are things you can't apologize for.

"Eliz…Betty, I'm not here about the past. I'm here about Dr. Bennett's murder."

"That doesn't have anything to do with me."

"It has to do with all of us. Dan Moore lives next door to you."

I don't say anything.

"He and Ceci and Jim Dyer and Tom Brunelli are the ringleaders in a secret organization to close Emerton Memorial Hospital. They think the hospital is a breeding ground for the infections resistant to every antibiotic except endozine. Well, they're right about that—all hospitals are. But Dan and his group are determined to punish any doctor who prescribes endozine, so that no organisms develop a resistance to it, too, and it's kept effective in case one of *them* needs it."

"Sylvia,"—the name tastes funny in my mouth, after all this time—"I'm telling you this doesn't have anything to do with me."

"And I'm telling you it does. We need you, Eliz…Betty. You live next door to Dan and Ceci. You can tell us when they leave the house, who comes to it, anything suspicious you see. We're not a vigilante group, Betty, like they are. We aren't doing anything illegal. We don't kill people, and we don't blow up bridges, and we don't threaten people like the Nordstrums who get endozine for their sick kids but are basically uneducated blue collar—"

She stops. Jack and I are basically uneducated blue collar. I say coldly, "I can't help you, Sylvia."

"I'm sorry, Betty. That wasn't what I meant. Look, this is more important than anything that happened a decade and a half ago! Don't you *understand*?" She leans toward me across the table. "The whole country's caught in this thing. It's already a public health crisis as big as the Spanish influenza epidemic of 1918, and it's only just started! Drug-resistant bacteria can produce a new generation every twenty minutes, they can swap resistant genes not only within a species but across *different* species. The bacteria are *winning*. And people like the Moores are taking advantage of that to contribute further to the breakdown of even basic social decency."

In high school Sylvia had been on the debating team. But so, in that other life, had I. "If the Moores' group is trying to keep endozine from being used, then aren't they also fighting against the development of more drug-resistant bacteria? And if that's so, aren't they the ones, not you, who are ultimately aiding the country's public health?"

"Through dynamiting. And intimidation. And murder. Betty, I know you don't approve of those things. I wouldn't be here telling you about our countergroup if I thought you did. Before I came here, we looked very carefully at you. At the kind of person you are. Are now. You and your husband are law-abiding people, you vote, you make a contribution to the Orphans of AIDS Fund, you—"

"How did you know about that? That's supposed to be a secret contribution!"

"—you signed the petition to protect the homeless from harassment. Your husband served on the jury that convicted Paul Keene of fraud, even though his real-estate scheme was so good for the economy of Emerton. You—"

"Stop it," I say. "You don't have any right to investigate me like I was some criminal!"

Only, of course, I was. Once. Not now. Sylvia's right about that—Jack and I believe in law and order, but for different reasons. Jack because that's what his father believed in, and his grandfather. Me, because I learned in Bedford that enforced rules are the only thing that even halfway restrains the kind of predators Sylvia James never dreamed of. The kind I want kept away from my children.

Sylvia says, "We have a lot of people on our side, Betty. People who don't want to see this town slide into the same kind of violence there is in Albany and Syracuse and, worst case, New York."

A month ago, New York Hospital in Queens was blown up. The whole thing, with a series of coordinated timed bombs. Seventeen hundred people dead in less than a minute.

"It's a varied group," she continues. "Some town leaders, some housewives, some teachers, nearly all the medical personnel at the hospital. All people who care what happens to Emerton."

"Then you've got the wrong person here," I say, and it comes out harsher than I want to reveal. "I don't care about Emerton."

"You have reasons," Sylvia says evenly. "And I'm part of your reasons, I know. But I think you'll help us, Elizabeth. I know you must be concerned about your son—we've all observed what a good mother you are."

So she brought up Sean's name first. I say, "You're wrong again, Sylvia. I don't need you to protect Sean, and if you've let him get involved in helping you, you'll wish you'd never been born. I've worked damn hard to make sure that what happened seventeen years ago never touches him. He doesn't need to get mixed up in any way with your 'medical personnel at the hospital.' And Sean sure the hell doesn't owe this town anything, there wasn't even anybody who would take him in after my aunt died, he had to go to—"

The look on her face stops me. Pure surprise. And then something else.

"Oh my God," she says. "Is it possible you don't know? Hasn't Sean told you?"

"Told me what?" I stand up, and I'm seventeen years old again, and just that scared. Sylvia-and-Elizabeth.

"Your son isn't helping our side. He's working for Dan Moore and Mike Dyer. They use juveniles because if they're caught, they won't be tried as severely as adults. We think Sean was one of the kids they used to blow up the bridge over the river."

I look first at the high school. Sean isn't there; he hadn't even shown up for homeroom. No one's home at his friend Tom's house, or at Keith's. He isn't at the Billiard Ball or the Emerton Diner or the American Bowl. After that, I run out of places to search.

This doesn't happen in places like Emerton. We have fights at basketball games and grand theft auto and smashed store windows on Halloween and sometimes a drunken tragic car crash on prom night. But not secret terrorists, not counter-terrorist vigilante groups. Not in Emerton.

Not with my son.

I drive to the factory and make them page Jack.

He comes off the line, face creased with sweat and dirt. The air is filled with clanging machinery and grinding drills. I pull him outside the door, where there are benches and picnic tables for workers on break. "Betty! What is it?"

"Sean," I gasp. "He's in danger."

Something shifts behind Jack's eyes. "What kind of danger?"

"Sylvia Goddard came to see me today. Sylvia James. She says Sean is involved with the group that blew up the bridge, the ones who are trying to get Emerton Memorial closed, and…and killed Dr. Bennett."

Jack peels off his bench gloves, taking his time. Finally he looks up at me. "How come that bitch Sylvia Goddard comes to you with this? After all this time?"

"Jack! Is that all you can think of? Sean is in trouble!"

He says gently, "Well, Bets, it was bound to happen sooner or later, wasn't it? He's always been a tough kid to raise. Rebellious. Can't tell him anything."

I stare at Jack.

"Some people just have to learn the hard way."

"Jack…this is serious! Sean might be involved in terrorism! He could end up in jail!"

"Couldn't ever tell him anything," Jack says, and I hear the hidden satisfaction in his voice, that he doesn't even know is there. Not his son. Dr. Randy Satler's son. Turning out bad.

"Look," Jack says, "when the shift ends I'll go look for him, Bets. Bring him home. You go and wait there for us." His face is gentle, soothing. He really will find Sean, if it's possible. But only because he loves me.

My sudden surge of hatred is so strong I can't even speak.

"Go on home, Bets. It'll be all right. Sean just needs to have the nonsense kicked out of him."

I turn and walk away. At the turning in the parking lot, I see Jack walking jauntily back inside, pulling on his gloves.

I drive home, because I can't think what else to do. I sit on the couch and reach back in my mind, for that other place, the place I haven't gone to since I got out of Bedford. The gray granite place that turns you to granite, too, so you can sit and wait for hours, for weeks, for years, without feeling very much. I go into that place, and I become the Elizabeth I was then, when Sean was in foster care someplace and I didn't know who had him or what they might be doing to him or how I would get him back. I go into the gray granite place to become stone.

And it doesn't work.

It's been too long. I've had Sean too long. Jack has made me feel too safe. I can't find the stony place.

Jackie is spending the night at a friend's. I sit in the dark, no lights on, car in the garage. Sean doesn't come home, and neither does Jack. At two in the morning, a lot of people in dark clothing cross the back lawn and quietly enter Dan and Ceci's house next door, carrying bulky packages wrapped in black cloth.

Jack staggers in at six-thirty in the morning. Alone. His face droops with exhaustion.

"I couldn't find him, Betty. I looked everywhere."

"Thank you," I say, and he nods. Accepting my thanks. This was something he did for me, not for Sean. Not for himself, as Sean's stepfather. I push down my sudden anger and say, "You better get some sleep."

"Right." He goes down the narrow hallway into our bedroom. In three minutes he's snoring.

I let the car coast in neutral down the driveway. Our bedroom faces the street. The curtains don't stir.

The West River Road is deserted, except for a few eighteen-wheelers. I cross the river at the interstate and start back along the east side. Three miles along, in the middle of farmland, the smell of burned flesh rolls in the window.

Cows, close to the pasture fence. I stop the car and get out. Fifteen or sixteen Holsteins. By straining over the fence, I can see the bullet holes in their heads. Somebody herded them together, shot them one by one, and started a half-hearted fire among the bodies with neatly cut firewood. The fire had gone out; it didn't look as if it was supposed to burn long. Just long enough to attract attention that hadn't come yet.

I'd never heard that cows could get human diseases. Why had they been shot?

I get back in my car and drive the rest of the way to Emerton Memorial.

This side of town is deathly quiet. Grass grows unmowed in yard after yard. One large, expensive house has old newspapers piled on the porch steps, ten or twelve of them. There are no kids waiting for school buses, no cars pulling out of driveways on the way to work. The hospital parking lot has huge empty stretches between cars. At the last minute I drive on through the lot, parking instead across the street in somebody's empty driveway, under a clump of trees.

Nobody sits at the information desk. The gift shop is locked. Nobody speaks to me as I study the directory on the lobby wall, even though two figures in gowns and masks hurry past. CHIEF OF MEDICINE, DR. RANDOLF SATLER. Third floor, east wing. The elevator is deserted.

It stops at the second floor. When the doors open a man stands there, a middle-aged farmer in overalls and work boots, his eyes red and swollen like he's been crying. There are tinted windows across from the elevators and I can see the back of him reflected in the glass. Coming and going. From somewhere I hear a voice calling, "Nurse, oh nurse, oh God…" A gurney sits in the hallway, the body on it covered by a sheet up to the neck. The man in overalls looks at me and raises both hands to ward off the elevator, like it's some kind of demon. He steps backward. The doors close.

I grip the railing on the elevator wall.

The third floor looks empty. Bright arrows lead along the hallways: yellow for PATHOLOGY and LAB SERVIC-ES, green for RESPIRATORY THERAPY, red for SUPPORT SERVICES. I follow the yellow arrow.

It dead-ends at an empty alcove with chairs, magazines thrown on the floor. And three locked doors off a short cor-ridor that's little more than an alcove.

I pick the farthest door and pound on it. No words, just regular blows of my fist. After a minute, I start on the sec-ond one. A voice calls, "Who's there?"

I recognize the voice, even through the locked door. Even after seventeen years. I shout, "Police! Open the door!"

And he does. The second it cracks, I shove it hard and push my way into the lab.

"*Elizabeth?*"

He's older, heavier, but still the same. Dark hair, blue eyes…I look at that face every day at dinner. I've looked at it at soccer matches, in school plays, in his playpen. Dr. Satler looks more shaken to see me than I would have thought, his face white, sweat on his forehead.

"Hello, Randy."

"Elizabeth. You can't come in here. You have to leave—"

"Because of the staph? Do you think I care about that? After all, I'm in the hospital, right, Randy? This is where the endozine is. This place is safe. Unless it gets blown up while I'm standing here."

He stares at my left hand, still gripping the doorknob behind me. Then at the gun in my right hand. A seventeen-year-old Smith & Wesson, and for five of those years the gun wasn't cleaned or oiled, hidden under my aunt's garage. But it still fires.

"I'm not going to shoot you, Randy. I don't care if you're alive or dead. But you're going to help me. I can't find my son,"—*your son*—"and Sylvia Goddard told me he's mixed up with that group that blew up the bridge. He's hiding with them someplace, probably scared out of his skull. You know everybody in town, everybody with power, you're going to get on that phone there and find out where Sean is."

"I would do that anyway," Randy says, and now he looks the way I remember him: impatient and arrogant. But not completely. There's still sweat on his pale face. "Put that stupid thing away, Elizabeth."

"No."

"Oh, for…" He turns his back on me and punches at the phone.

"Cam? Randy Satler here. Could you…no, it's not about that…No. Not yet."

Cameron Witt. The mayor. His son is chief of Emerton's five cops.

"I need a favor. There's a kid missing…I know that, Cam. You don't have to lecture *me* on how bad delay could…But you might know about this kid. Sean Baker."

"Pulaski. Sean Pulaski." He doesn't even know that.

"Sean Pulaski. Yeah, that one…okay. Get back to me…I told you. *Not yet*." He hangs up. "Cam will hunt around and call back. Now will you put that stupid gun away, Elizabeth?"

"You still don't say thank you for anything." The words just come out. Fuck, fuck, fuck.

"To Cam, or to you for not shooting me?" He says it evenly, and the evenness is the only way I finally see how furious he is. People don't order around Dr. Randy Satler at gunpoint. A part of my mind wonders why he doesn't call security.

I say, "All right, I'm here. Give me a dose of endozine, just in case."

He goes on staring at me with that same level, furious gaze. "Too late, Elizabeth."

"What do you mean, too late? Haven't you got endozine?"

"Of course we do." Suddenly he staggers slightly, puts out one hand behind him, and holds onto a table covered with glassware and papers.

"Randy. You're sick."

"I am. And not with anything endozine is going to cure. Ah, Elizabeth, why didn't you just phone me? I'd have looked for Sean for you."

"Oh, right. Like you've been so interested and helpful in raising him."

"You never asked me."

I see that he means it. He really believes his total lack of contact with his son is my fault. I see that Randy gives only what he's asked to. He waits, lordly, for people to plead for his help, beg for it, and then he gives it. If it suits him.

I say, "I'll bet anything your kids with your wife are turning out really scary."

The blood rushes to his face, and I know I guessed right. His blue eyes darken and he looks like Jack looks just before Jack explodes. But Randy isn't Jack. An explosion would be too clean for him. He says instead, "You were stupid to come here. Haven't you been listening to the news?"

I haven't.

"The CDC publicly announced just last night what medical personnel have seen for weeks. A virulent strain of staphylococcus aureus has incorporated endozine-resistant plasmids from enterococcus." He pauses to catch his breath. "And pneumococcus may have done the same thing."

"What does that mean?"

"It means, you stupid woman, that now there are highly contagious infections that we have no drugs to cure. No antibiotics at all, not even endozine. This staph is resistant to them all. And it can live everywhere."

I lower the gun. The empty parking lot. No security to summon. The man who wouldn't get on the elevator. And Randy's face. "And you've got it."

"We've all got it. Everyone…in the hospital. And for forcing your way in here, you probably do, too."

"You're going to die," I say, and it's half a hope.

And he *smiles*.

He stands there in his white lab coat, sweating like a horse, barely able to stand up straight, almost shot by a woman he'd once abandoned pregnant, and he smiles. His blue eyes gleam. He looks like a picture I once saw in a book, back when I read a lot. It takes me a minute to re-member that it was my high school World History book. A picture of some general.

"Everybody's going to die eventually," Randy says. "But not me right now. At least…I hope not." Casually he crosses the floor toward me, and I step backward. He smiles again.

"I'm not going to deliberately infect you, Elizabeth. I'm a *doctor*. I just want the gun."

"No."

"Have it your way. Look, how much do you know about the bubonic plague of the fourteenth century?"

"Nothing," I say, although I do. Why had I always acted stupider around Randy than I actually am?

"Then it won't mean anything to you to say that this mutated staph has at least that much potential"—again he paused and gulped air—"for rapid and fatal transmission. It flourishes everywhere. Even on doorknobs."

"So why the fuck are you *smiling*?" Alexander. That was the picture of the general. Alexander the Great.

"Because I...because the CDC distributed...I was on the national team to discover..." His face changes again. Goes even whiter. And he pitches over onto the floor.

I grab him, roll him face up, and feel his forehead. He's burning up. I bolt for the door. "Nurse! Doctor! There's a sick doctor here!"

Nobody comes.

I run down the corridors. Respiratory Therapy is empty. So is Support Services. I jab at the elevator button, but before it comes I run back to Randy.

And stand above him, lying there crumpled on the floor, laboring to breathe.

I'd dreamed about a moment like this for years. Dreamed it waking and asleep, in Emerton and in Bedford Hills and in Jack's arms. Dreamed it in a thousand ridiculous melodramatic versions. And here it is, Randy helpless and pleading, and me strong, standing over him, free to walk away and let him die. Free.

I wring out a towel in cold water and put it on his forehead. Then I find ice in the refrigerator in a corner of the lab and substitute that. He watches me, his breathing wheezy as old machinery.

"Elizabeth. Bring me...syringe in a box on...that table."

I do it. "Who should I get for you, Randy? Where?"

"Nobody. I'm not…as bad…as I sound. Yet. Just the initial…dyspnea." He picks up the syringe.

"Is there medicine for you in there? I thought you said endozine wouldn't work on this new infection." His color is a little better now.

"Not medicine. And not for me. For you."

He looks at me steadily. And I see that Randy would never plead, never admit to helplessness. Never ever think of himself as helpless.

He lowers the hand holding the syringe back to the floor. "Listen, Elizabeth. You have…almost certainly have…"

Somewhere, distantly, a siren starts to wail. Randy ignores it. All of a sudden his voice becomes much firmer, even though he's sweating again and his eyes burn bright with fever. Or something.

"This staph is resistant to everything we can throw at it. We cultured it and tried. Cephalosporins and aminoglycosides and vancomycin, even endozine…I'll go into gram-positive septic shock…" His eyes glaze, but after a moment he seems to find his thought again. "We exhausted all points of counterattack. Cell wall, bacterial ribosome, folic acid pathway. Microbes just evolve countermeasures. Like beta-lactamase."

I don't understand this language. Even talking to himself, he's making me feel stupid again. I ask something I do understand.

"Why are people killing cows? Are the cows sick, too?"

He focuses again. "Cows? No, they're not sick. Farmers use massive doses of antibiotics to increase meat and milk production. Agricultural use of endozine has increased the rate of resistance development by over a thousand percent since—Elizabeth, this is irrelevant! Can't you pay attention to what I'm saying for three minutes?"

I stand up and look down at him, lying shivering on the floor. He doesn't even seem to notice, just keeps on lecturing.

"But antibiotics weren't invented by humans. They were invented by the microbes themselves to use…against each other and…they had two billion years of evolution at it before we even showed up…We should have—where are you going?"

"Home. Have a nice life, Randy."

He says quietly, "I probably will. But if…you leave now, you're probably dead. And your husband and kids, too."

"Why? Damn it, stop lecturing and tell me why!"

"Because you're infected, and there's no antibiotic for it, but there *is* another bacteria that will attack the drug-resistant staph."

I look at the syringe in his hand.

"It's a Trojan horse plasmid. That's a…never mind. It can get into the staph in your blood and deliver a lethal gene. One that will kill the staph. It's an incredible discovery. But the only way to deliver it so far is to deliver the whole bacteria."

My knees all of a sudden get shaky. Randy watches me from his position on the floor. He looks shakier himself. His breathing turns raspier again.

"No, you're not sick yet, Elizabeth. But you will be."

I snap, "From the staph germs or from the cure?"

"Both."

"You want to make me sicker. With two bacteria. And hope one will kill the other."

"Not hope. I *know*. I actually saw…it on the electromicrograph…" His eyes roll, refocus. "…could package just the lethal plasmid on a transpon if we had time…no time. Has to be the whole bacteria." And then, stronger, "The CDC team is working on it. But *I* actually caught it on the electromicrograph!"

I say, before I know I'm going to, "Stop congratulating yourself and give me the syringe. Before you die."

I move across the floor toward him, put my arms around him to prop him in a sitting position against the table leg. His whole body feels on fire. But somehow he keeps his hands steady as he injects the syringe into the inside of my elbow. While it drains sickness into me I say, "You never actually wanted me, did you, Randy? Even before Sean?"

"No," he says. "Not really." He drops the syringe.

I bend my arm. "You're a rotten human being. All you care about is yourself and your work."

He smiles the same cold smile. "So? My work is what matters. In a larger sense than you could possibly imagine. You were always a weak sentimentalist, Elizabeth. Now, go home."

"Go *home*? But you said…"

"I said you'd infect everyone. And you will—with the bacteria that attacks staph. It should cause only a fairly mild illness. Jenner…smallpox…"

"But you said I have the mutated staph, too!"

"You almost certainly do. Yes…And so will everyone else, before long. Deaths…in New York State alone…passed one million this morning. Six and a half percent of the… the population…Did you really think you could hide on your side of…the…river…"

"Randy!"

"Go…home."

I strip off his lab coat and wad it up for a pillow, bring more ice from the refrigerator, try to get him to drink some water.

"Go…home. Kiss everybody." He smiles to himself, and starts to shake with fever. His eyes close.

I stand up again. Should I go? Stay? If I could find someone in the hospital to take care of him—

The phone rings. I seize it. "Hello? Hello?"

"Randy? Excuse me, can I talk to Dr. Satler? This is Cameron Witt."

I try to sound professional. "Dr. Satler can't come to the phone right now. But if you're calling about Sean Pulaski, Dr. Satler asked me to take the message."

"I don't…oh, all right. Just tell Randy the Pulaski boy is with Richard and Sylvia James. He'll understand." The line clicks.

I replace the receiver and stare at Randy, fighting for breath on the floor, his face as gray as Sean's when Sean realized it was murder he'd gotten involved with. No, not as gray. Because Sean had been terrified, and Randy is only sick.

My work is what matters.

But how had Sean known to go to Sylvia? Even if he knew from Ceci who was on the other side, how did he know which people would hide him, would protect him when I could not, Jack could not? Sylvia-and-Elizabeth. How much did Sean actually know about the past I'd tried so hard to keep from touching him?

I reach the elevator, my finger almost touching the button, when the first explosion rocks the hospital.

It's in the west wing. Through the windows opposite the elevator banks I see windows in the far end of the building explode outward. Thick greasy black smoke billows out the holes. Alarms begin to screech.

Don't touch the elevators. Instructions remembered from high school, from grade-school fire drills. I race along the hall to the fire stairs. What if they put a bomb in the stairwell? What if *who* put a bomb in the stairwell? *A lot of people in dark clothing cross the back lawn and quietly enter Dan and Ceci's house next door, carrying bulky packages wrapped in black cloth.*

A last glimpse through a window by the door to the fire stairs. People are running out of the building, not many, but the ones I see are pushing gurneys. A nurse staggers outside, three small children in her arms, on her hip, clinging to her back.

They aren't setting off any more bombs until people have a chance to get out.

I let the fire door close. Alarms scream. I run back to Pathology and shove open the heavy door.

Randy lies on the floor, sweating and shivering. His lips move but if he's muttering aloud, I can't hear it over the alarm. I tug on his arm. He doesn't resist and he doesn't help, just lies like a heavy dead cow.

There are no gurneys in Pathology. I slap him across the face, yelling "Randy! Randy! Get up!" Even now, even here, a small part of my mind thrills at hitting him.

His eyes open. For a second, I think he knows me. It goes away, then returns. He tries to get up. The effort is enough to let me hoist him over my shoulder in a fireman's carry. I could never have carried Jack, but Randy is much slighter, and I'm very strong.

But I can't carry him down three flights of stairs. I get him to the top, prop him up on his ass, and shove. He slides down one flight, bumping and flailing, and glares at me for a minute. "For…God's sake…Janet!"

His wife's name. I don't think about this tiny glimpse of his marriage. I give him another shove, but he grabs the railing and refuses to fall. He hauls himself—I'll never know how—back to a sitting position, and I sit next to him. Together, my arm around his waist, tugging and pulling, we both descend the stairs the way two-year-olds do, on our asses. Every second I'm waiting for the stairwell to blow up. Sean's gray face at dinner: *Fucking vigilantes'll get us all.*

The stairs don't blow up. The fire door at the bottom gives out on a sidewalk on the side of the hospital away from both street and parking lot. As soon as we're outside, Randy blacks out.

This time I do what I should have done upstairs and grab him under the armpits. I drag him over the grass as far as I can. Sweat and hair fall in my eyes, and my vision keeps blurring. Dimly I'm aware of someone running toward us.

"It's Dr. Satler! Oh my God!"

A man. A large man. He grabs Randy and hoists him over his shoulder, a fireman's carry a lot smoother than mine, barely glancing at me. I stay behind them and, at the first buildings, run in a wide loop away from the hospital.

My car is still in the deserted driveway across the street. Fire trucks add their sirens to the noise. When they've torn past, I back my car out of the driveway and push my foot to the floor, just as a second bomb blows in the east wing of the hospital, and then another, and the air is full of flying debris as thick and sharp as the noise that goes on and on and on.

Three miles along the East River Road, it suddenly catches up with me. All of it. I pull the car off the road and I can't stop shaking. Only a few trucks pass me, and nobody stops. It's twenty minutes before I can start the engine again, and there has never been a twenty minutes like them in my life, not even in Bedford. At the end of them, I pray that there never will be again.

I turn on the radio as soon as I've started the engine.

"—in another hospital bombing in New York City, St. Clare's Hospital in the heart of Manhattan. Beleaguered police officials say that a shortage of available officers make impossible the kind of protection called for by Mayor Thomas Flanagan. No group has claimed credit for the bombing, which caused fires that spread to nearby businesses and at least one apartment house.

"Since the Centers for Disease Control's announcement last night of a widespread staphylococcus resistant to endozine, and its simultaneous release of an emergency counter-

bacteria in twenty-five metropolitan areas around the country, the violence has worsened in every city transmitting
reliable reports to Atlanta. A spokesperson for the national
team of pathologists and scientists responsible for the dras-
tic countermeasure released an additional set of guidelines
for its use. The spokesperson declined to be identified, or
to identify any of the doctors on the team, citing fear of
reprisals if—"

A burst of static. The voice disappears, replaced by a
shrill hum.

I turn the dial carefully, looking for another station with
news.

By the time I reach the west side of Emerton, the streets
are deserted. Everyone has retreated inside. It looks like the
neighborhoods around the hospital look. Had looked. My
body still doesn't feel sick.

Instead of going straight home, I drive the deserted
streets to the Food Mart.

The parking lot is as empty as everywhere else. But the
basket is still there, weighted with stones. Now the stones
hold down a pile of letters. The top one is addressed in blue
Magic Marker: TO DR. BENNETT. The half-buried wine
bottle holds a fresh bouquet, chrysanthemums from somebody's garden. Nearby a foot-high American flag sticks in
the ground, beside a white candle on a styrofoam plate, a
stone crucifix, and a Barbie doll dressed like an angel. Saran
Wrap covers a leather-bound copy of *The Prophet*. There are
also five anti-NRA stickers, a pile of seashells, and a bat-
tered peace sign on a gold chain like a necklace. The peace
sign looks older than I am.

When I get home, Jack is still asleep.

I stand over him, as a few hours ago I stood over Randy
Satler. I think about how Jack visited me in prison, week
after week, making the long drive from Emerton even in

the bad winter weather. About how he'd sit smiling at me through the thick glass in the visitors' room, his hands with their grease-stained fingers resting on his knees, smiling even when we couldn't think of anything to say to each other. About how he clutched my hand in the delivery room when Jackie was born, and the look on his face when he first held her. About the look on his face when I told him Sean was missing: the sly, secret, not-my-kid triumph. And I think about the two sets of germs in my body, readying for war.

I bend over and kiss Jack full on the lips.

He stirs a little, half wakes, reaches for me. I pull away and go into the bathroom, where I use his toothbrush. I don't rinse it. When I return, he's asleep again.

I drive to Jackie's school, to retrieve my daughter. Together, we will go to Sylvia Goddard's—Sylvia James's—and get Sean. I'll visit with Sylvia, and shake her hand, and kiss her on the cheek, and touch everything I can. When the kids are safe at home, I'll visit Ceci and tell her I've thought it over and I want to help fight the overuse of antibiotics that's killing us. I'll touch her, and anyone else there, and everyone that either Sylvia or Ceci introduces me to, until I get too sick to do that. If I get that sick. Randy said I wouldn't, not as sick as he is. Of course, Randy has lied to me before. But I have to believe him now, on this.

I don't really have any choice. Yet.

A month later, I am on my way to Albany to bring back another dose of the counterbacteria, which the news calls "a reengineered prokaryote." They're careful not to call it a germ.

I listen to the news every hour now, although Jack doesn't like it. Or anything else I'm doing. I read, and I study, and now I know what prokaryotes are, and beta-lactamase, and plasmids. I know how bacteria fight to survive, evolving whatever they need to wipe out the competition and go on producing the next generation. That's all that matters to bacteria. Survival by their own kind.

And that's what Randy Satler meant, too, when he said, "My work is what matters." Triumph by his own kind. It's what Ceci believes, too. And Jack.

We bring in the reengineered prokaryotes in convoys of cars and trucks, because in some other places there's been trouble. People who don't understand, people who won't understand. People whose family got a lot sicker than mine. The violence isn't over, even though the CDC says the epidemic itself is starting to come under control.

I'm early. The convoy hasn't formed yet. We leave from a different place in town each time. This time we're meeting behind the American Bowl. Sean is already there, with Sylvia. I take a short detour and drive, for the last time, to the Food Mart.

The basket is gone, with all its letters to the dead man. So are the American flag and the peace sign. The crucifix is still there, but it's broken in half. The latest flowers in the wine bottle are half wilted. Rain has muddied the Barbie doll's dress, and her long blonde hair is a mess. Someone ripped up the anti-NRA stickers. The white candle on a styrofoam plate and the pile of seashells are untouched.

We are not bacteria. More than survival matters to us, or should. The individual past, which we can't escape, no matter how hard we try. The individual present, with its unsafe choices. The individual future. And the collective one.

I search in my pockets. Nothing but keys, money clip, lipstick, tissues, a blue marble I must have stuck in my pocket when I cleaned behind the couch. Jackie likes marbles.

I put the marble beside the candle, check my gun, and drive to join the convoy for the city.

FAULT LINES

"If the truth shall kill them, let them die."
—Immanuel Kant

THE FIRST DAY OF SCHOOL, we had assault-with-intent in Ms. Kelly's room. I was in my room next door, 136, laying down the law to 7C math. The usual first-day bullshit: turn in homework every day, take your assigned seat as soon as you walk in, don't bring a weapon or an abusive attitude into my classroom or you'll wish you'd never been born. The kids would ignore the first, do the others—for me anyway. Apparently not for Jenny Kelly.

"Mr. Shaunessy! Mr. Shaunessy! Come quick, they throwing chairs next door! The new teacher crying!" A pretty, tiny girl I recognized from last year: Lateesha Jefferson. Her round face glowed with excitement and satisfaction. A riot! Already! On the very first day!

I looked over my class slowly, penetratingly, letting my gaze linger on each upturned face. I took my time about it. Most kids dropped their eyes. Next door, something heavy hit the wall. I lowered my voice, so everybody had to strain to hear me.

"Nobody move while I'm gone. You all got that?"

Some heads nodded. Some kids stared back, uncertain but cool. A few boys smirked and I brought my unsmiling gaze to their faces until they stopped. Shouts filtered through the wall.

"Okay, Lateesha, tell Ms. Kelly I'm coming." She took off like a shot, grinning, Paul Revere in purple leggings and silver shoes.

I limped to the door and turned for a last look. My students all sat quietly, watching me. I saw Pedro Valesquez and Steven Cheung surreptitiously scanning my jacket for the bulge of a service revolver that of course wasn't there. My reputation had become so inflated it rivaled the NYC budget. In the hall Lateesha screamed in a voice that could have deafened rock stars, "Mr. Shaunessy coming! You ho's better stop!"

In 134, two eighth-grade girls grappled in the middle of the floor. For a wonder, neither seemed to be armed, not even with keys. One girl's nose streamed blood. The other's blouse was torn. Both screamed incoherently, nonstop, like stuck sirens. Kids raced around the room. A chair had apparently been hurled at the chalkboard, or at somebody once standing in front of the chalkboard; chair and board had cracked. Jenny Kelly yelled and waved her arms. Lateesha was wrong; Ms. Kelly wasn't crying. But neither was she helping things a hell of a lot. A few kids on the perimeter of the chaos saw me and fell silent, curious to see what came next.

And then I saw Jeff Connors, leaning against the window wall, arms folded across his chest, and his expression as he watched the fighting girls told me everything I needed to know.

I took a huge breath, letting it fill my lungs. I bellowed at top volume, and with no facial expression whatsoever, "Freeze! Now!"

And everybody did.

The kids who didn't know me looked instantly for the gun and the back-up. The kids who did know me grinned,

stifled it, and nodded slightly. The two girls stopped pound-
ing each other to twist toward the noise—my bellow had
shivered the hanging fluorescents—which was time enough
for me to limp across the floor, grab the girl on top, and haul
her to her feet. She twisted to swing on me, thought better
of it, and stood there, panting.

The girl on the floor whooped, leaped up, and tensed to
slug the girl I held. But then she stopped. She didn't know
me, but the scene had alerted her: nobody yelling anymore,
the other wildcat quiet in my grip, nobody racing around
the room. She glanced around, puzzled.

Jeff still leaned against the wall.

They expected me to say something. I said nothing, just
stood there, impassive. Seconds dragged by. Fifteen, thirty,
forty-five. To adults, that's a long time. To kids, it's forever.
The adrenaline ebbs away.

A girl in the back row sat down at her desk.

Another followed.

Pretty soon they were all sitting down, quiet, not exactly
intimidated but interested. This was different, and different was cool. Only the two girls were left, and Jeff Connors leaning on the window, and a small Chinese kid whose
chair was probably the one hurled at the chalkboard. I saw
that the crack ran right through words printed neatly in
green marker:

Ms. Kelly
English 8E

After a minute, the Chinese kid without a chair sat on
his desk.

Still I said nothing. Another minute dragged past. The
kids were uneasy now. Lateesha said helpfully, "Them girls
supposed to go to the nurse, Mr. Shaunessy. Each one by
they own self."

I kept my grip on the girl with the torn blouse. The other girl, her nose gushing blood, suddenly started to cry. She jammed her fist against her mouth and ran out of the room.

I looked at each face, one at a time.

Eventually I released my grip on the second girl and nodded at Lateesha. "You go with her to the nurse."

Lateesha jumped up eagerly, a girl with a mission, the only one I'd spoken to. "You come on, honey," she said, and led away the second girl, clucking at her under her breath.

Now they were all eager for the limelight. Rosaria said quickly, "They fighting over Jeff, Mr. Shaunessy."

"No they ain't," said a big, muscled boy in the second row. He was scowling. "They fighting cause Jonelle, she dissed Lisa."

"No, they—"

Everybody had a version. They all jumped in, intellectuals with theories, arguing with each other until they saw I wasn't saying anything, wasn't trying to sort through it, wasn't going to participate. One by one, they fell silent again, curious.

Finally Jeff himself spoke. He looked at me with his absolutely open, earnest, guileless expression and said, "It was them suicides, Mr. Shaunessy."

The rest of the class looked slightly confused, but willing to go along with this. They knew Jeff. But now Ms. Kelly, excluded for five full minutes from her own classroom, jumped in. She was angry. "*What* suicides? What are you talking about, uh…"

Jeff didn't deign to supply his name. She was supposed to know it. He spoke directly to me. "Them old people. The ones who killed theirselves in that hospital this morning. And last week. In the newspaper."

I didn't react. Just waited.

"You know, Mr. Shaunessy," Jeff went on, in that same open, confiding tone. "Them old people shooting and hanging and pushing theirselves out of windows. At their age. In their sixties and seventies and eighties." He shook his head regretfully.

The other kids were nodding now, although I'd bet my pension none of them ever read anything in any newspaper.

"It just ain't no example to us," Jeff said regretfully. "If even the people who are getting three good meals a day and got people waiting on them and don't have to work or struggle no more with the man—if *they* give up, how we supposed to think there's anything in this here life for us?"

He leaned back against the window and grinned at me: triumphant, regretful, pleading, an inheritor of a world he hadn't made. His classmates glanced at each other sideways, glanced at me, and stopped grinning.

"A tragedy, that's what it is," Jeff said, shaking his head. ' 'A tragedy. All them old people, deciding a whole life just don't make it worth it to stick to the rules. How *we* supposed to learn to behave?"

"You have to get control of Jeff Connors," I told Jenny Kelly at lunch in the faculty room. This was an exposed-pipes, flaking-plaster oasis in the basement of Benjamin Franklin Junior High. Teachers sat jammed together on folding metal chairs around brown formica tables, drinking coffee and eating out of paper bags. Ms. Kelly had plopped down next to me and practically demanded advice. "That's actually not as hard as it might look. Jeff's a hustler, an operator, and the others follow him. But he's not uncontrollable."

"Easy for you to say," she retorted, surprising me. "They look at you and see the macho ex-cop who weighs what? Two-thirty? Who took out three criminals before you got shot, and has strong juice at Juvenile Hall. They look at me and see a five-foot-three, one-hundred-twenty-pound nobody they can all push around. Including Jeff."

"So don't let him," I said, wondering how she'd heard all the stories about me so fast. She'd only moved into the district four days ago.

She took a healthy bite of her cheese sandwich. Although she'd spent the first half of the lunch period in the ladies' room, I didn't see any tear marks. Maybe she fixed her makeup to cover tear stains. Margie used to do that. Up close Jenny Kelly looked older than I'd thought at first: twenty-eight, maybe thirty. Her looks weren't going to make it any easier to control a roomful of thirteen-year-old boys. She pushed her short blond hair off her face and looked directly at me.

"Do you really carry a gun?"

"Of course not. Board of Education regs forbid any weapons by anybody on school property. You know that."

"The kids think you carry."

I shrugged.

"And you don't tell them otherwise."

I shrugged again.

"Okay, I can't do that either," she said. "But I'm not going to fail at this, Gene. I'm just not. You're a big success here, everybody says so. So tell me what I *can* do to keep enough control of my classes that I have a remote chance of actually teaching anybody anything."

I studied her, and revised my first opinion, which was that she'd be gone by the end of September. No tear stains, not fresh out of college, able to keep eating under stress. The verbal determination I discounted; I'd heard a lot of verbal determination from rookies when I was on the Force, and most of it melted away three months out of Police Academy. Even sooner in the City School District.

"You need to do two things," I said. "First, recognize that these kids can't do without connection to other human beings. Not for five minutes, not for one minute. They're starved for it. And to most of them, 'connection' means arguing, fighting, struggling, even abuse. It's what they're used to, and it's what they'll naturally create, because it feels better to them than existing alone in a social vacuum for even a minute. To compete with that, to get them to disengage from each other long enough to listen to you, you have to give them an equally strong connection to *you*. It doesn't have to be intimidation, or some bullshit fantasy about going up against the law. You can find your own way. But unless you're a strong presence—very strong, very distinctive—of one kind or another, they're going to ignore you and go back to connecting with each other."

"Connection," she said, thinking about it. "What about connecting to the material? English literature has some pretty exciting stuff in it, you know."

"I'll take your word for it. But no books are exciting to most of these kids. Not initially. They can only connect to the material through a person. They're that starved."

She took another bite of sandwich. "And the second thing?"

"I already told you. Get control of Jeff Connors. Immediately."

"Who is he? And what was all that bullshit about old people killing themselves?"

I said, "Didn't you see it on the news?"

"Of course I did. The police are investigating, aren't they? But what did it have to do with my classroom?"

"Nothing. It was a diversionary tactic. A cover-up."

"Of what?"

"Could be a lot of things. Jeff will use whatever he hears to confuse and mislead, and he hears everything. He's bright, unmotivated, a natural leader, and—unbelievably—not a gang member. You saw him—no big gold, no beeper. His police record is clean. So far, anyway."

Jenny said, "You worked with him a little last year."

"No, I didn't work with him. I controlled him in class, was all." She'd been asking about me.

"So if *you* didn't really connect with him, how do I?"

"I can't tell you that," I said, and we ate in silence for a few minutes. It didn't feel strained. She looked thoughtful, turning over what I'd told her. I wondered suddenly whether she'd have made a good cop. Her ears were small, I noticed, and pink, with tiny gold earrings in the shape of little shells.

She caught me looking, and smiled, and glanced at my left hand.

So whoever she'd asked about me hadn't told her everything. I gulped my last bite of sandwich, nodded, and went back to my room before 7H came thundering up the stairs, their day almost over, one more crazy period where Mr. Shaunessy actually expected them to pay attention to some weird math instead of their natural, intense, contentious absorption in each other.

Two more elderly people committed suicide, at the Angels of Mercy Nursing Home on Amsterdam Avenue.

I caught it on the news, while correcting 7H's first-day quiz to find out how much math they remembered from last year. They didn't remember squat. My shattered knee was propped up on the hassock beside the bones and burial tray of a Hungry Man Extra-Crispy Fried Chicken.

"…identified as Giacomo della Francesca, seventy-eight, and Lydia Smith, eighty. The two occupied rooms on the same floor, according to nursing home staff, and both had been in fairly good spirits. Mrs. Smith, a widow, threw herself from the roof of the eight-story building. Mr. della Francesca, who was found dead in his room, had apparently stabbed himself. The suicides follow very closely on similar deaths this morning at the Beth Israel Retirement Home on West End Avenue. However, Captain Michael Doyle, NYPD, warned against premature speculation about—"

I shifted my knee. This Captain Doyle must be getting nervous; this was the third pair of self-inflicted fatalities in nursing homes within ten days. Old people weren't usually susceptible to copy-cat suicides. Pretty soon the *Daily News* or the *Post* would decide that there was actually some nut running around Manhattan knocking off the elderly. Or that there was a medical conspiracy backed by Middle East terrorists and extraterrestrials. Whatever the tabloids chose, the NYPD would end up taking the blame.

Suddenly I knew, out of nowhere, that Margie was worse.

I get these flashes like that, out of nowhere, and I hate it. I never used to. I used to know things the way normal people know things, by seeing them or reading them or hearing them or reasoning them through. Ways that made sense. Now, for the last year, I get these flashes of knowing things some other way, thoughts just turning up in my mind, and the intuitions are mostly right. Mostly right, and nearly always bad.

This wasn't one of my nights to go to the hospital. But I flicked off the TV, limped to the trash to throw away my dinner tray, and picked up the cane I use when my leg has been under too much physical stress. The phone rang. I paused to listen to the answering machine, just in case it was Libby calling from Cornell to tell me about her first week of classes.

"Gene, this is Vince Romano." Pause. "Bucky." Pause. "I know it's been a long time."

I sat down slowly on the hassock.

"Listen, I was sorry to hear about Margie. I was going to…you were…it wasn't.…" Despite myself, I had to grin. People didn't change. Bucky Romano never could locate a complete verb.

He finished floundering. "…to say how sorry I am. But that's not why I'm calling." Long pause. "I need to talk to you. It's important. Very important." Pause. "It's not about

Father Healey again, or any of that old...something else entirely." Pause. "Very important, Gene. I can't...it isn't... you won't..." Pause. Then his voice changed, became stronger. "I can't do this alone, Gene."

Bucky had never been able to do anything alone. Not when we were six, not when we were eleven, not when we were seventeen, not when he was twenty-three and it wasn't any longer me but Father Healey who decided what he did. Not when he was twenty-seven and it was me again deciding for him, more unhappy about that than I'd ever been about anything in my life until Margie's accident.

Bucky recited his phone number, but he didn't hang up. I could hear him breathing. Suddenly I could almost see him, somewhere out there, sitting with the receiver pressed so close to his mouth that it would look like he was trying to swallow it. Hoping against hope that I might pick up the phone after all. Worrying the depths of his skinny frantic soul for what words he could say to make me do this.

"Gene...it's about...I shouldn't say this, but after all you're a...were a...it's about those elderly deaths." Pause. "I work at Kelvin Pharmaceuticals now." And then the click.

What the hell could anybody make of any of that?

I limped to the elevator and caught a cab to St. Clare's Hospital.

Margie *was* worse, although the only way I could tell was that there was one more tube hooked to her than there'd been last night. She lay in bed in the same position she'd lain in for eighteen months and seven days: curled head to knees, splinter-thin arms bent at the elbows. She weighed ninety-nine pounds. Gastrostomy and catheter tubes ran into her, and now an IV drip on a pole as well. Her beautiful brown hair, worn away a bit at the back of her head from constant contact with the pillow, was dull. Its sheen, like her life, had faded deep inside its brittle shafts, unrecoverable.

"Hello, Margie. I'm back."

I eased myself into the chair, leg straight out in front of me.

"Libby hasn't called yet. First week of classes, schedule to straighten out, old friends to see—you know how it is." Margie always had. I could see her and Libby shopping the week before Libby's freshman year, laughing over the Gap bags, quarreling over the price of something I'd buy either of them now, no matter what it cost. Anything.

"It's pretty cool out for September, sweetheart. But the leaves haven't changed yet. I walked across the Park just yesterday—all still green. Composing myself for today. Which wasn't too bad. It's going to be a good school year, I think."

Have a great year! Margie always said to me on the first day of school, as if the whole year would be compressed in that first six hours and twenty minutes. For three years she'd said it, the three years since I'd been retired from the Force and limped into a career as a junior-high teacher. I remembered her standing at the door, half-dressed for her secretarial job at Time-Warner, her silk blouse stretched across those generous breasts, the slip showing underneath. *Have a great day! Have a great five minutes!*

"Last-period 7H looks like a zoo, Margie. But when doesn't last period look like a zoo? They're revved up like Ferraris by then. But both algebra classes look good, and there's a girl in 7A whose transcript is incredible. I mean, we're talking future Westinghouse Talent winner here."

Talk to her, the doctor had said. *We don't know what coma patients can and cannot hear.* That had been a year and a half ago. Nobody ever said it to me now. But I couldn't stop.

"There's a new sacrificial lamb in the room next to mine, eighth-grade English. She had a cat fight in there today. But I don't know, she might have more grit than she looks. And guess who called. Bucky Romano. After all this time.

Thirteen years. He wants me to give him a call. I'm not sure yet."

Her teeth gapped and stuck out. The anti-seizure medication in her gastrostomy bag made the gum tissue grow too much. It displaced her teeth.

"I finally bought curtains for the kitchen. Like Libby nagged me to. Although they'll probably have to wait until she comes home at Thanksgiving to get hung. Yellow. You'd like them."

Margie had never seen this kitchen. I could see her in the dining room of the house I'd sold, up on a chair hanging drapes, rubbing at a dirty spot on the window....

"Gene?"

"Hi, Susan." The shift nurse looked as tired as I'd ever seen her. "What's this new tube in Margie?"

"Antibiotics. She was having a little trouble breathing, and an X-ray showed a slight pneumonia. It'll clear right up on medication. Gene, you have a phone call."

Something clutched in my chest. *Libby*. Ever since that '93 Lincoln had torn through a light on Lexington while Margie crossed with a bag of groceries, any phone call in an unexpected place does that to me. I limped to the nurses' station.

"Gene? This is Vince. Romano. Bucky."

"Bucky."

"I'm sorry to bother you at...I was so sorry to hear about Margie, I left a message on your machine but maybe you haven't been home to...listen, I need to see you, Gene. It's important. Please."

"It's late, Bucky. I have to teach tomorrow. I teach now, at—"

"*Please*. You'll know why when I see you. I have to see you."

I closed my eyes. "Look, I'm pretty tired. Maybe another time."

"*Please*, Gene. Just for a few minutes. I can be at your place in fifteen minutes!"

Bucky had never minded begging. I remembered that, now. Suddenly I didn't want him to see where I lived, how I lived, without Margie. What I really wanted was to tell him "no."

But I couldn't. I never had, not our whole lives, and I couldn't now—why not? I didn't know.

"All right, Bucky. A few minutes. I'll meet you in the lobby here at St. Clare's."

"Fifteen minutes. God, thanks, Gene. Thanks so much, I really appreciate it, I need to—"

"*Okay.*"

"See you soon."

He didn't mind begging, and he made people help him. Even Father Healey had found out that. Coming in to Bucky's life, and going out.

The lobby of St. Clare's never changed. Same scuffed green floor, slashed gray vinyl couches mended with wide tape, information-desk attendant who looked like he could have been a bouncer at Madison Square Garden. Maybe he had. Tired people yelled and whispered in Spanish, Greek, Korean, Chinese. Statues of the Madonna and St. Clare and the crucified Christ beamed a serenity as alien here as money.

Bucky and I grew up in next-door apartments in a neighborhood like this one, a few blocks from Our Lady of Perpetual Sorrows. That's how we defined our location: "two doors down from the crying Broad." We made our First Communion together, and our Confirmation, and Bucky was best man when I married Marge. But by that time he'd entered the seminary, and any irreverence about Our Lady had disappeared, along with all other traces of humor, humility, or humanity. Or so I thought then. Maybe

I wasn't wrong. Even though he always made straight A's in class, Bucky-as-priest-in-training was the same as Bucky-as-shortstop or Bucky-as-third-clarinet or Bucky-as-altar-boy: intense, committed, short-sightedly wrong.

He'd catch a high pop and drop it. He'd know "Claire de Lune" perfectly, and be half a beat behind. Teeth sticking out, skinny face furrowed in concentration, he'd bend over the altar rail and become so enraptured by whatever he saw there that he'd forget to make the response. We boys would nudge each other and grin, and later howl at him in the parking lot.

But his decision to leave the priesthood wasn't a howler. It wasn't even a real decision. He vacillated for months, growing thinner and more stuttery, and finally he'd taken a bottle of pills and a half pint of vodka. Father Healey and I found him, and had his stomach pumped, and Father Healey tried to talk him back into the seminary and the saving grace of God. From his hospital bed Bucky had called me, stuttering in his panic, to come get him and take him home. He was terrified. Not of the hospital—of Father Healey.

And I had, coming straight from duty, secure in my shield and gun and Margie's love and my beautiful young daughter and my contempt for the weakling who needed a lapsed-Catholic cop to help him face an old priest in a worn-out religion. God, I'd been smug.

"Gene?" Bucky said. "Gene Shaunessy?"

I looked up at the faded lobby of St. Clare's.

"Hello, Bucky."

"God, you look…I can't…you haven't changed a bit!"

Then he started to cry.

I got him to a Greek place around the corner on Ninth. The dinner trade was mostly over and we sat at a table in the shadows, next to a dirty side window with a view of a brick alley, Bucky with his back to the door. Not that he cared if anybody saw him crying. I cared. I ordered two beers.

"Okay, what is it?"

He blew his nose and nodded gratefully. "Same old Gene. You always just...never any..."

"Bucky. What the fuck is wrong?"

He said, unexpectedly, "You hate this."

Over his shoulder, I eyed the door. Starting eighteen months ago, I'd had enough tears and drama to last me the rest of my life, although I wasn't going to tell Bucky that. If he didn't get it over with....

"I work at Kelvin Pharmaceuticals," Bucky said, suddenly calmer. "After I left the seminary, after Father Healey...you remember..."

"Go on," I said, more harshly than I'd intended. Father Healey and I had screamed at each other outside Bucky's door at St. Vincent's, while Bucky's stomach was being pumped. I'd said things I didn't want to remember.

"I went back to school. Took a B.S. in chemistry. Then a Ph.D. You and I, about that time of...I wanted to call you after you were shot but...I could have tried harder to find you earlier, I know...anyway. I went to work for Kelvin, in the research department. Liked it. I met Tommy. We live together."

He'd never said. But, then, he'd never had to. And there hadn't been very much saying anyway, not back then, and certainly not at Our Lady of Perpetual Sorrows.

"I liked the work at Kelvin. Like it. Liked it." He took a deep breath. "I worked on Camineur. You take it, don't you, Gene?"

I almost jumped out of my skin. "How'd you know that?"

He grinned. "Not by any medical record hacking. Calm down, it isn't...people can't tell. I just guessed, from the profile."

He meant *my* profile. Camineur is something called a neurotransmitter uptake-regulator. Unlike Prozac and the other antidepressants that were its ancestors, it fiddles not just with serotonin levels but also with norepinephrine and dopamine and a half dozen other brain chemicals. It was prescribed for me after Marge's accident. Non-addictive, no bad side effects, no dulling of the mind. Without it, I couldn't sleep, couldn't eat, couldn't concentrate. Couldn't stop wanting to kill somebody every time I walked into St. Clare's.

I had found myself in a gun shop on Avenue D, trigger-testing a nine-millimeter, which felt so light in my hand it floated. When I looked at the thoughts in my head, I went to see Margie's doctor.

Bucky said, quietly for once, "Camineur was designed to prevent violent ideation in people with strong but normally controlled violent impulses, whose control has broken down under severe life stress. It's often prescribed for cops. Also military careerists and doctors. Types with compensated paranoia restrained by strong moral strictures. Nobody told you that the Camineur generation of mood inhibitors was that specific?"

If they did, I hadn't been listening. I hadn't been listening to much in those months. But I heard Bucky now. His hesitations disappeared when he talked about his work.

"It's a good drug, Gene. You don't have to feel…there isn't anything shameful about taking it. It just restores the brain chemistry to whatever it was before the trauma."

I scowled, and gestured for two more beers.

"All right. I didn't mean to…There's been several generations of neural pharmaceuticals since then. And that's why I'm talking to you."

I sipped my second beer, and watched Bucky drain his.

"Three years ago we…there was a breakthrough in neuropharm research, really startling stuff, I won't go into the…

we started a whole new line of development. I was on the team. Am. On the team."

I waited. Sudden raindrops, large and sparse, struck the dirty window.

"Since Camineur, we've narrowed down the effects of neuropharms spectacularly. I don't know how much you know about this, but the big neurological discovery in the last five years is that repeated intense emotion doesn't just alter the synaptic pathways in the brain. It actually changes your brain structure from the cellular level up. With any intense experience, new structures start to be built, and if the experience is repeated, they get reinforced. The physical changes can make you, say, more open to risk-taking, or calmer in the face of stress. Or the physical structures that get built can make it hard or even impossible to function normally, even if you're trying with all your will. In other words, your life literally makes you crazy."

He smiled. I said nothing.

"What we've learned is how to affect only those pathways created by depression, only those created by fear, only those created by narcissistic rage...we don't touch your memories. They're there. You can see them, in your mind, like billboards. But now you drive past them, not through them. In an emotional sense."

Bucky peered at me. I said, not gently, "So what pills do *you* take to drive past your memories?"

He laughed. "I don't." I stayed impassive but he said hastily anyway, "Not that people who do are...it isn't a sign of weakness to take neuropharms, Gene. Or a sign of strength not to. I just...it isn't...I was waiting, was all. I was waiting."

"For what? Your prince to come?" I was still angry.

He said simply, "Yes."

Slowly I lowered my beer. But Bucky returned to his background intelligence.

"This drug my team is working on now...the next step was to go beyond just closing down negative pathways. Take, as just one example, serotonin. Some researcher said... there's one theory that serotonin, especially, is like cops. Having enough of it in your cerebral chemistry keeps riots and looting and assault in the brain from getting out of control. But just holding down crime doesn't, all by itself, create prosperity or happiness. Or joy. For that, you need a new class of neuropharms that create positive pathways. Or at least strengthen those that are already there."

"Cocaine," I said. "Speed. Gin and tonic."

"No, no. Not a rush of power. Not a temporary high. Not temporary at all, and not isolating. The neural pathways that make people feel...the ones that let you..." He leaned toward me, elbows on the table. "Weren't there moments, Gene, when you felt so close to Margie it was like you crawled inside her skin for a minute? Like you *were* Margie?"

I looked at the window. Raindrops slid slowly down the dirty glass, streaking it dirtier. In the alley, a homeless man prowled the garbage cans. "What's this got to do with the elderly suicides? If you have a point to make, make it."

"They weren't suicides. They were murders."

"Murders? Some psycho knocking off old people? What makes you think so?"

"Not some psycho. And I don't think so. I *know*."

"How?"

"All eight elderlies were taking J-24. That's the Kelvin code name for the neuropharm that ends situational isolation. It was a clinical trial."

I studied Bucky, whose eyes burned with Bucky light: intense, pleading, determined, inept. And something else, something that hadn't been there in the old days. "Bucky, that makes no sense. The NYPD isn't perfect, God knows, but they can tell the difference between suicide and murder. And anyway, the suicide rate rises naturally among old people, they get depressed—" I stopped. He had to already know this.

"That's just it!" Bucky cried, and an old Greek couple at a table halfway across the room turned to stare at him. He lowered his voice. "The elderly in the clinical trial *weren't* depressed. They were very carefully screened for it. No psychological, chemical, or social markers for depression. These were the…when you see old people in travel ads, doing things, full of life and health, playing tennis and dancing by candlelight…the team psychologists looked for our clinical subjects very carefully. *None* of them was depressed!"

"So maybe your pill made them depressed. Enough to kill themselves."

"No! No! J-24 couldn't…there wasn't any…it didn't make them depressed. I saw it." He hesitated. "And besides…"

"Besides what?"

He looked out at the alley. A waiter pushed a trolley of dirty dishes past our table. When Bucky spoke again, his voice sounded odd.

"I gave five intense years to J-24 and the research that led to it, Gene. Days, evenings, weekends—eighty hours a week in the lab. Every minute until I met Tommy, and maybe too much time even after that. I know everything that the Kelvin team leaders know, everything that can be known about that drug's projected interaction with existing neurotransmitters. J-24 was my life."

As the Church had once been. Bucky couldn't do anything by halves. I wondered just what his position on "the team" had actually been.

He said, "We designed J-24 to combat the isolation that even normal, healthy people feel with age. You get old. Your friends die. Your mate dies. Your children live in another state, with lives of their own. All the connections you built up over decades are gone, and in healthy people, those connections created very thick, specific, strong neural structures. Any new friends you make in a nursing home or retirement community—there just aren't the years left to duplicate the strength of those neural pathways. Even when outgoing, undepressed, risk-taking elderlies try."

I didn't say anything.

"J-24 was specific to the neurochemistry of connection. You took it in the presence of someone else, and it opened the two of you up to each other, made it possible to genuinely—*genuinely*, at the permanent chemical level—imprint on each other."

"You created an *aphrodisiac for geezers*?"

"No," he said, irritated. "Sex had nothing to do with it. Those impulses originate in the limbic system. This was... emotional bonding. Of the most intense, long-term type. Don't tell me all you ever felt for Margie was sex!"

After a minute he said, "I'm sorry."

"Finish your story."

"It *is* finished. We gave the drug to four sets of volunteers, all people who had long-term terminal diseases but weren't depressed, people who were willing to take risks in order to enhance the quality of their own perceptions in the time left. I was there observing when they took it. They bonded like baby ducks imprinting on the first moving objects they see. No, not like that. More like...like..." He looked over my shoulder, at the wall, and his eyes filled with water. I glanced around to make sure nobody noticed.

"Giacomo della Francesca and Lydia Smith took J-24 together almost a month ago. They were transformed by this incredible joy in each other. In knowing each other. Not each other's memories, but each other's...souls. They talked, and held hands, and you could just feel that they were completely open to each other, without all the psychological defenses we use to keep ourselves walled off. They knew each other. They almost *were* each other."

I was embarrassed by the look on his face. "But they didn't know each other like that, Bucky. It was just an illusion."

"No. It wasn't. Look, what happens when you connect with someone, share something intense with them?"

I didn't want to have this conversation. But Bucky didn't really need me to answer; he rolled on all by himself, unstoppable.

"What happens when you connect is that you exhibit greater risk-taking, with fewer inhibitions. You exhibit greater empathy, greater attention, greater receptivity to what is being said, greater pleasure. And *all* of those responses are neurochemical, which in turn create, reinforce, or diminish physical structures in the brain. J-24 just reverses the process. Instead of the experience causing the neurochemical response, J-24 supplies the physical changes that create the experience. And that's not all. The drug boosts the *rate* of structural change, so that every touch, every word exchanged, every emotional response, reinforces neural pathways one or two hundred times as much as a normal life encounter."

I wasn't sure how much of this I believed. "And so you say you gave it to four old couples…does it only work on men and women?"

A strange look passed swiftly over his face: secretive, almost pained. I remembered Tommy. "That's all who have tried it so far. Can you…have you ever thought about what it would be like to be really merged, to know him—to be him—think of it, Gene! I could—"

"I don't want to hear about that," I said harshly. Libby would hate that answer. My liberal, tolerant daughter. But I'd been a cop. Lingering homophobia went with the territory, even if I wasn't exactly proud of it. Whatever Bucky's fantasies were about him and Tommy, I didn't want to know.

Bucky didn't look offended. "All right. But just imagine— an end to the terrible isolation that we live in our whole tiny lives…." He looked at the raindrops sliding down the window.

"And you think somebody murdered those elderly for that? Who? Why?"

"I don't know."

"Bucky. Think. This doesn't make any sense. A drug company creates a…what did you call it? A neuropharm. They get it into clinical trials, under FDA supervision—"

"No," Bucky said.

I stared at him.

"It would have taken years. Maybe decades. It's too radical a departure. So Kelvin—"

"You knew there was no approval."

"Yes. But I thought…I never thought…" He looked at me, and suddenly I had another one of those unlogical flashes, and I saw there was more wrong here even than Bucky was telling me. He believed that he'd participated, in whatever small way, in creating a drug that led someone to murder eight old people. Never mind if it was true—Bucky believed it. He believed this same company was covering its collective ass by calling the deaths depressive suicides, when they could not have been suicides. And yet Bucky sat in front of me without chewing his nails to the knuckles, or pulling out his hair, or hating himself. Bucky, to whom guilt was the staff of life.

I'd seen him try to kill himself over leaving the Church. I'd watched him go through agonies of guilt over ignoring answering-machine messages from Father Healey. Hell, I'd watched him shake and cry because at ten years old we'd stolen three apples from a market on Columbus Avenue. Yet there he sat, disturbed but coherent. For Bucky, even serene. Believing he'd contributed to murder.

I said, "What neuropharms do you take, Bucky?"

"I told you. None."

"None at all?"

"No." His brown eyes were completely honest. "Gene, I want you to find out how these clinical subjects really died. You have access to NYPD records—"

"Not anymore."

"But you *know* people. And cases get buried there all the time, you used to tell me that yourself, with enough money you can buy yourself an investigation unless somebody high up in the city is really out to get you. Kelvin Pharmaceuticals doesn't have those kinds of enemies. They're not the Mob. They're just…"

"Committing murder to cover up an illegal drug trial? I don't buy it, Bucky."

"Then find out what *really* happened."

I shot back, "What do *you* think happened?"

"I don't know! But I do know this drug is a good thing! Don't you understand, it holds out the possibility of a perfect, totally open connection with the person you love most in the world.…Find out what happened, Gene. It wasn't suicide. J-24 doesn't cause depression. I *know* it. And for this drug to be denied people would be…it would be a sin."

He said it so simply, so naturally, that I was thrown all over again. This wasn't Bucky, as I had known him. Or maybe it was. He was still driven by sin and love.

I stood and put money on the table. "I don't want to get involved in this, Bucky. I really don't. But—one thing more—"

"Yeah?"

"Camineur. Can it…does it account for…" Jesus, I sounded like him. "I get these flashes of intuition about things I've been thinking about. Sometimes it's stuff I didn't know."

He nodded. "You knew the stuff before. You just didn't know you knew. Camineur strengthens intuitive right-brain pathways. As an effect of releasing the stranglehold of violent thoughts. You're more distanced from compulsive thoughts of destruction, but also more likely to make connections among various non-violent perceptions. You're just more intuitive, Gene, now that you're less driven."

And I'm less Gene, my unwelcome intuition said. I gazed down at Bucky, sitting there with his skinny fingers splayed on the table, an unBucky-like serenity weirdly mixed with his manic manner and his belief that he worked for a corporation that had murdered eight people. Who the hell was *he*?

"I don't want to get involved in this," I repeated.

"But you will," Bucky said, and in his words I heard utter, unshakable faith.

Jenny Kelly said, "I set up a conference with Jeff Connors and he never showed." It was Friday afternoon. She had deep circles around her eyes. Raccoon eyes, we called them. They were the badge of teachers who were new, dedicated, or crazy. Who sat up until 1:00 A.M. in a frenzy of lesson planning and paper correcting, and then arrived at school at 6:30 A.M. to supervise track or meet with students or correct more papers.

"Set up another conference," I suggested. "Sometimes by the third or fourth missed appointment, guilt drives them to show up."

She nodded. "Okay. Meanwhile, Jeff has my class all worked up over something called the Neighborhood Safety Information Network, where they're supposed to inform on their friends' brothers' drug activity, or something. It's somehow connected to getting their Social Services checks. It's got the kids all in an uproar...I sent seventeen kids to the principal in three days."

"You might want to ease up on that, Jenny. It gives everybody—kids and administration—the idea that you can't control your own classroom."

"I can't," she said, so promptly and honestly that I had to smile. "But I *will*."

"Well, good luck."

"Listen, Gene, I'm picking the brains of everybody I can get to talk to me about this. Want to go have a cup of coffee someplace?"

"Sorry."

"Okay." She didn't look rebuffed, which was a relief. Today her earrings matched the color of her sweater. A soft blue, with lace at the neck. "Maybe another time."

"Maybe." It was easier than an outright no.

Crossing the parking lot to my car, I saw Jeff Connors. He slapped me a high-five. "Ms. Kelly's looking for you, Jeff."

"She is? Oh, yeah. Well, I can't today. Busy."

"So I hear. There isn't any such thing as the Neighborhood Safety Information Network, is there?"

He eyed me carefully. "Sure there is, Mr. S."

"Really? Well, I'm going to be at Midtown South station house this afternoon. I'll ask about it."

"It's, like, kinda new. They maybe don't know nothing about it yet."

"Ah. Well, I'll ask anyway. See you around, Jeff."

"Hang loose."

He watched my car all the way down the block, until I turned the corner.

The arrest room at Midtown South was full of cops filling out forms: fingerprint cards, On-line Booking System Arrest Worksheets, complaint reports, property invoices, requests for laboratory examinations of evidence, Arrest Documentation Checklists. The cops, most of whom had changed out of uniform, scribbled and muttered and sharpened pencils. In the holding pen alleged criminals cursed and slept and muttered and sang. It looked like fourth-period study hall in the junior-high cafeteria.

I said, "Lieutenant Fermato?"

A scribbling cop in a Looney Tunes sweatshirt waved me toward an office without even looking up.

"Oh my God. Gene Shaunessy. Risen from the fuckin' dead."

"Hello, Johnny."

"Come *in*. God, you look like a politician. Teaching must be the soft life."

"Better to put on a few pounds than look like a starved rat."

We stood there clasping hands, looking at each other, not saying the things that didn't need saying anyway, even if we'd had the words, which we didn't. Johnny and I had been partners for seven years. We'd gone together through foot pursuits and high-speed chases and lost files and violent domestics and bungled traps by Internal Affairs and robberies-in-progress and the grueling boredom of the street. Johnny's divorce. My retirement. Johnny had gone into Narcotics a year before I took the hit that shattered my knee. If he'd been my partner, it might not have happened. He'd made lieutenant only a few months ago. I hadn't seen him in a year and a half.

Suddenly I knew—or the Camineur knew—why I'd come to Midtown South to help Bucky after all. I'd already lost too many pieces of my life. Not the life I had now—the life I'd had once. My real one.

"Gene—about Marge…"

I held up my hand. "Don't. I'm here about something else. Professional."

His voice changed. "You in trouble?"

"No. A friend is." Johnny didn't know Bucky; they'd been separate pieces of my old life. I couldn't picture them in the same room together for more than five minutes. "It's about the suicides at the Angels of Mercy Nursing Home. Giacomo della Francesca and Lydia Smith."

Johnny nodded. "What about it?"

"I'd like to see a copy of the initial crime-scene report."

Johnny looked at me steadily. But all he said was, "Not my jurisdiction, Gene."

I looked back. If Johnny didn't want to get me the report, he wouldn't. But either way, he *could*. Johnny'd been the best undercover cop in Manhattan, mostly because he was so good at putting together his net of criminal informers, inside favors, noncriminal spies, and unseen procedures. I didn't believe he'd dismantled any of it just because he'd come in off the street. Not Johnny.

"Is it important?"

I said, "It's important."

"All right," he said, and that was all that had to be said. I asked him instead about the Neighborhood Safety Information Network.

"We heard about that one," Johnny said. "Pure lies, but somebody's using it to stir up a lot of anti-cop crap as a set-up for something or other. We're watching it."

"Watches run down," I said, because it was an old joke between us, and Johnny laughed. Then we talked about old times, and Libby, and his two boys, and when I left, the same cops were filling out the same forms and the same perps were still sleeping or cursing or singing, nobody looking at each other in the whole damn place.

By the next week, the elderly suicides had disappeared from the papers, which had moved on to another batch of mayhem and alleged brutality in the three-oh. Jenny Kelly had two more fights in her classroom. One I heard through the wall and broke up myself. The other Lateesha told me about in the parking lot. "That boy, Mr. Shaunessy, that Richie Tang, he call Ms. Kelly an ugly bitch! He say she be sorry for messing with *him*!"

"And then what?" I said, reluctantly.

Lateesha smiled. "Ms. Kelly, she yell back that Richie might act like a lost cause but he ain't lost to *her*, and she be damned if anybody gonna talk to her that way. But Richie just smile and walk out. Ms. Kelly, she be gone by Thanksgiving."

"Not necessarily," I said. "Sometimes people surprise you."

"Not me, they don't."

"Maybe even you, Lateesha."

Jenny Kelly's eyes wore permanent rings: sleeplessness, anger, smudged mascara. In the faculty room she sat hunched over her coffee, scribbling furiously with red pen on student compositions. I found myself choosing a different table.

"Hi, Gene," Bucky's voice said on my answering machine. "Please call if you…I wondered whether you found out any… give me a call. Please. I have a different phone number, I'll give it to you." Pause. "I've moved."

I didn't call him back. Something in the "I've moved" hinted at more pain, more complications, another chapter in Bucky's messy internal drama. I decided to call him only if I heard something from Johnny Fermato.

Who phoned me the following Tuesday, eight days after my visit to Midtown South. "Gene. John Fermato."

"Hey, Johnny."

"I'm calling to follow through on our conversation last week. I'm afraid the information you requested is unavailable."

I stood in my minuscule kitchen, listening to the traffic three stories below, listening to Johnny's cold formality. "Unavailable?"

"Yes. I'm sorry."

"You mean the file has disappeared? Been replaced by a later version? Somebody's sitting on it?"

"I'm sorry, the information you requested isn't available."

"Right," I said, without expression.

"Catch you soon."

"Bye, Lieutenant."

After he hung up I stood there holding the receiver, surprised at how much it hurt. It was a full five minutes before the anger came. And then it was distant, muffled. Filtered through the Camineur, so that it wouldn't get out of hand.

Safe.

Jeff Connors showed up at school after a three-day absence, wearing a beeper, and a necklace of thick gold links.

"Jeff, he big now," Lateesha told me, and turned away, lips pursed like the disapproving mother she would someday be.

I was patrolling the hall before the first bell when Jenny Kelly strode past me and stopped at the door to the boys' room, which wasn't really a door but a turning that hid the urinals and stalls from obvious view. The door itself had been removed after the fifth wastebasket fire in two days. Jeff came around the corner, saw Ms. Kelly, and stopped. I could see he was thinking about retreating again, but her voice didn't let him. "I want to see you, Jeff. In my free period." Her voice said he would be there.

"Okay," Jeff said, with no hustle, and slouched off, beeper riding on his hip.

I said to her, "He knows when your free period is."

She looked at me coolly. "Yes."

"So you've gotten him to talk to you."

"A little." Still cool. "His mother disappeared for three days. She uses. She's back now, but Jeff doesn't trust her to take care of his little brother. Did you even know he had a little brother, Gene?"

I shook my head.

"Why not?" She looked like Lateesha. Disapproving mother. The raccoon eyes were etched deeper. "This boy is in trouble, and he's one we don't have to lose. We can still save him. *You* could have, last year. He admires you. But you never gave him the time of day, beyond making sure he wasn't any trouble to *you*."

"I don't think you have the right to judge whether–"

"Don't I? Maybe not. I'm sorry. But don't you see, Jeff only wanted from you—"

"That's the bell. Good luck today, Ms. Kelly."

She stared at me, then gave me a little laugh. "Right. And where were *you* when the glaciers melted? Never mind." She walked into her classroom, which diminished in noise only a fraction of a decibel.

Her earrings were little silver hoops, and her silky blouse was red.

After school I drove to the Angels of Mercy Nursing Home and pretended I was interested in finding a place for my aging mother. A woman named Karen Gennaro showed me a dining hall, bedrooms, activity rooms, a little garden deep in marigolds and asters, nursing facilities. Old people peacefully played cards, watched TV, sat by sunshiny windows. There was no sign that eighty-year-old Lydia Smith had thrown herself from the roof, or that her J-24-bonded boyfriend Giacomo della Francesca had stabbed himself to death.

"I'd like to walk around a little by myself now," I told Ms. Gennaro. "Just sort of get the feel of the place. My mother is…particular." She hesitated. "We don't usually allow—"

"Mom didn't like Green Meadows because too many corridors were painted pale blue and she hates pale blue. She rejected Saint Anne's because the other women didn't care enough about their hairdos and so the atmosphere wasn't self-respecting. She wouldn't visit Havenview because there was no piano in the dining room. This is the tenth place I've reported on."

She laughed. "No wonder you sound so weary. All right, just check out with me before you leave."

I inspected the day room again, chatting idly with a man watching the weather channel. Then I wandered to the sixth floor, where Lydia Smith and Giacomo della Francesca had lived. I chatted with an elderly man in a wheelchair, and a sixteen-year-old Catholic Youth volunteer, and a Mrs. Locurzio, who had the room on the other side of Lydia Smith's. Nothing.

A janitor came by mopping floors, a heavy young man with watery blue eyes and a sweet, puzzled face like a bearded child.

"Excuse me—have you worked here long?"

"Four years." He leaned on his mop, friendly and shy.

"Then you must come to know the patients pretty well."

"Pretty well." He smiled. "They're nice to me."

I listened to his careful, spaced speech, a little thick on each initial consonant. "Are all of them nice to you?"

"Some are mean. Because they're sick and they hurt."

"Mrs. Smith was always nice to you."

"Oh, yes. A nice lady. She talked to me every day." His doughy face became more puzzled. "She died."

"Yes. She was unhappy with her life."

He frowned. "Mrs. Smith was unhappy? But she…no. She was happy." He looked at me in appeal. "She was *always* happy. Aren't you her friend?"

"Yes," I said. "I just made a mistake about her being unhappy."

"She was *always* happy. With Mr. Frank. They laughed and laughed and read books."

"Mr. della Francesca."

"He said I could call him Mr. Frank."

I said, "What's your name?"

"Pete," he said, as if I should know it.

"Oh, you're Pete! Yes, Mrs. Smith spoke to me about you. Just before she died. She said you were nice, too."

He beamed. "She was my friend."

"You were sad when she died, Pete."

"I was sad when she died."

I said, "What exactly happened?"

His face changed. He picked up the mop, thrust it into the rolling bucket. "Nothing."

"Nothing? But Mrs. Smith is dead."

"I gotta go now." He started to roll the bucket across the half-mopped floor, but I placed a firm hand on his arm. There's a cop intuition that has nothing to do with neuropharms.

I said, "Some bad people killed Mrs. Smith."

He looked at me, and something shifted behind his pale blue gaze.

"They didn't tell you that, I know. They said Mrs. Smith killed herself. But you know she was very happy and didn't do that, don't you? What did you see, Pete?"

He was scared now. Once, a long time ago, I hated myself for doing this to people like Pete. Then I got so I didn't think about it. It didn't bother me now, either.

"Mrs. Gennaro killed Mrs. Smith," I said.

Shock wiped out fear. "No, she didn't! She's a nice lady!"

"I say Mrs. Gennaro and the doctor killed Mrs. Smith."

"You're crazy! You're an asshole! Take it back!"

"Mrs. Gennaro and the doctor—"

"Mrs. Smith and Mr. Frank was all alone together when they went up to that roof!"

I said swiftly, "How do you know?"

But he was panicked now, genuinely terrified. Not of me—of what he'd said. He opened his mouth to scream. I said, "Don't worry, Pete. I'm a cop. I work with the cops you talked to before. They just sent me to double-check your story. I work with the same cops you told before."

"With Officer Camp?"

"That's right," I said. "With Officer Camp."

"Oh." He still looked scared. "I told them already! I told them I unlocked the roof door for Mrs. Smith and Mr. Frank like they asked me to!"

"Pete—"

"I gotta go!"

"Go ahead, Pete. You did good."

He scurried off. I left the building before he could find Karen Gennaro.

A call to an old friend at Records turned up an Officer Joseph Camphausen at Midtown South, a Ralph Campogiani in the Queens Robbery Squad, a Bruce Campinella at the two-four, and a detective second grade Joyce Campolieto in Intelligence. I guessed Campinella, but it didn't matter which one Pete had talked to, or that I wouldn't get another chance inside Angels of Mercy. I headed for West End Avenue.

The sun was setting. Manhattan was filled with river light. I drove up the West Side Highway with the window down, and remembered how much Margie had liked to do that, even in the winter. *Real air, Gene. Chilled like good beer*.

Nobody at the Beth Israel Retirement Home would talk to me about the two old people who died there, Samuel Fetterolf and Rose Kaplan. Nor would they let me wander around loose after my carefully guided tour. I went to the Chinese restaurant across the street and waited.

From every street-side window in Beth Israel I'd seen them head in here: well-dressed men and women visiting their parents and aunts and grandmothers after work. They'd stay an hour, and then they'd be too hungry to go home and cook, or maybe too demoralized to go home without a drink, a steady stream of overscheduled people dutifully keeping up connections with their old. I chose a table in the bar section, ordered, and ate slowly. It took a huge plate of moo goo gai pan and three club sodas before I heard it.

"How can you *say* that? She's not senile, Brad! She knows whether her friends are suicidal or not!"

"I didn't say she–"

"Yes, you did! You said we can't trust her perceptions! She's only old, not stupid!" Fierce thrust of chopsticks into her sweet and sour. She was about thirty, slim and tanned, her dark hair cut short. Preppy shirt and sweater. He wasn't holding up as well, the paunch and bald spot well underway, the beleaguered husband look not yet turned resentful.

"Joanne, I only said–"

"You said we should just discount what Grams said and leave her there, *even though* she's so scared. You always discount what she says!"

"I don't. I just—"

"Like about that thing at Passover. What Grams wanted was completely reasonable, and you just—"

"Excuse me," I said, before they drifted any more. The thing at Passover wouldn't do me any good. "I'm sorry, but I couldn't help but overhear. I have a grandmother in Beth Israel, too, and I'm a little worried about her, otherwise I wouldn't interrupt, it's just that…my grandmother is scared to stay there, too."

They inspected me unsmilingly, saying nothing.

"I don't know what to do," I said desperately. "She's never been like this."

"I'm sorry," Brad said stiffly, "we can't help."

"Oh, I understand. Strangers. I just thought…you said something about your grandmother being frightened…I'm sorry." I got up to leave, projecting embarrassment.

"Wait a minute," Joanne said. "What did you say your name was?"

"Aaron Sanderson."

"Joanne, I don't think—"

"Brad, if he has the same problem as—Mr. Sanderson, what is your grandmother afraid of? Is she usually nervous?"

"No, that's just it," I said, moving closer to their table. Brad frowned at me. "She's never nervous or jittery, and never depressed. She's fantastic, actually. But ever since those two residents died…"

"Well, that's just *it*," Joanne said. Brad sighed and shifted his weight. "Grams was friendly with Mrs. Kaplan, and she told me that Mrs. Kaplan would never in a million years commit suicide. She just *wouldn't*."

"Same thing my grandmother said. But I'm sure there couldn't be actual danger in Beth Israel," I said. Dismiss what the witness said and wait for the contradiction.

"Why not?" Joanne said. "They could be testing some new medication…in fact, Grams said Mrs. Kaplan had volunteered for some clinical trial. She had cancer."

Brad said, "And so naturally she was depressed. Or maybe depression was a side effect of the drug. You read about that shit all the time. The drug company will be faced with a huge lawsuit, they'll settle, they'll stop giving the pills, and everybody's grandmother is safe. That simple."

"No, smartie." Joanne glared at him. "It's not that simple. Grams said she spent the afternoon with Mrs. Kaplan a week or so *after* she started the drug. Mrs. Kaplan was anything but depressed. She was really up, and she'd fallen in love with Mr. Fetterolf who was also in the trial, and his daughter-in-law Dottie was telling me–"

"Joanne, let's go," Brad said. "I don't really feel like arguing here."

I said, "My grandmother knew Mr. Fetterolf slightly. And she's worried about his suicide—"

"So am *I*," Joanne said. "I keep telling and telling Brad—"

"Joanne, I'm going. You do what the hell you want."

"You can't just—all right, all right! Everything has to be your way!" She flounced up, threw me an apologetic look, and followed her husband out.

There were four Fetterolfs in the Manhattan phone directory. Two were single initials, which meant they were probably women living alone. I chose Herman Fetterolf on West Eighty-sixth.

The apartment building was nice, with a carpeted lobby and deep comfortable sofas. I said to the doorman, "Please tell Mrs. Dottie Fetterolf that there's a private investigator to talk to her about her father-in-law's death. My name is Joe Carter. Ask her if she'll come down to the lobby to talk to me."

He gave me a startled look and conveyed the message. When Mrs. Fetterolf came down, I could see she was ready to be furious at somebody, anybody. Long skirt swishing, long vest flapping, she steamed across the lobby. "You the private investigator? Who are you working for?"

"I'm not at liberty to say, Mrs. Fetterolf. But it's someone who, like you, has lost an elderly relative to suicide."

"Suicide! Ha! It wasn't any suicide! It was murder!"

"Murder?"

"They killed him! And no one will admit it!"

"What makes you think so?"

"Think? *Think?* I don't have to think, I *know*! One week he's fine, he's friends with this Mrs. Kaplan, they play Scrabble, they read books together, he's happy as a clam. Maybe even a little something gets going between them, who am I to say, more power to them. And then on the same night— the *same* night—he hangs himself and she walks in front of a bus! Coincidence? I don't think so!…Besides, there would be a note."

"I beg your—"

"My father-in-law would have left a note. He was thoughtful that way. You know what I'm saying? He wrote everybody in the whole family all the time, nobody could even keep up with reading it all. He would have left a note for sure."

"Did he—"

"He was lonely after his wife died. Sarah. A saint. They met fifty-six years ago—"

In the end, she gave me her father-in-law's entire history. Also Rose Kaplan's. I wrote it all down.

When I called Johnny Fermato, I was told by a wary desk sergeant that Lieutenant Fermato would get back to me.

In my dreams.

"Somebody's being screwed over, Margie," I said. "And it's probably costing somebody else pay-off money."

She lay there in the fetal position, her hands like claws. She was still connected by tubes to the humidified air supply, the catheter bag, the feeding pump. The pump made soft noises: *ronk, ronk*. I laid my briefcase on the bottom of her bed, which Susan would probably object to.

"It wasn't depression," I said to Margie. "Della Francesca and Mrs. Smith went up to that roof together. Alone together. Samuel Fetterolf and Rose Kaplan were in love." J-24 chemically induced love.

The bag in Margie's IV slowly emptied. The catheter bag slowly filled. Her ears were hidden under the dry, brittle, lifeless hair.

"Johnny Fermato knows something. Maybe only that the word's been passed down to keep the case closed. I did get the coroners' reports. They say 'self-inflicted fatal wounds.' All eight reports."

Somewhere in the hospital corridors, a woman screamed. Then stopped.

"Margie," I heard myself saying, "I don't want to come here anymore."

The next second, I was up and limping around the room. I put my forehead against the wall and ground it in. How could I say that to her? Margie, the only woman I'd ever loved, the person in the world I was closest to....On our wedding night, which was also her nineteenth birthday, she'd told me she felt like she could die from happiness. And I'd known what she meant.

And on that other night eight years later, when Bucky had done his pills-and-vodka routine, Margie had been with me when the phone rang. *Gene…Gene…I did it….*

Did what? Jesus, Bucky, it's after midnight—

But I don't…Father Healey…

Bucky, I gotta start my shift at eight tomorrow morning. Good night.

Gene, who's calling at this hour?

…say…good-bye….

Of all the inconsiderate…the phone woke Libby!

Tell Father Healey I never would have made…good priests don't doubt like…I can't touch God anymore….

And then I'd known. I was out of the apartment in fifteen seconds. Shoes, pants, gun. In my pajama top I drove to the seminary, leaned on the bell. Bucky wasn't there, but Father Healey was. I searched the rooms, the chapel, the little meditation garden, all the while traffic noises drowning out the thumping in my chest. Father Healey shouting questions at me. I wouldn't let him in my car. Get away from me you bastard you killed him, you and your insistence on pushing God on a mind never tightly wrapped in the first place…Bucky wasn't at his mother's house. Now I had two people screaming at me.

I found him at Our Lady of Perpetual Sorrows. Where I should have looked first. He'd broken a stained glass window, just smashed it with a board, no subtlety. He was in front of the altar, breathing shallow, already unconscious. EMS seemed to take forever to get there. The on-duty cops were faster; the stained-glass was alarm-wired.

But when it was over, Bucky's stomach pumped, sleeping it off at St. Vincent's, I had crawled back in bed next to Margie. Libby asleep in her little bedroom. I'd put my arms around my wife, and I'd vowed that after Bucky got out of the hospital, I'd never see him and his messy stupid dramas of faith again.

"I didn't mean that," I said to Margie, inert in her trach collar. "Sweetheart, I didn't mean it. Of course I want to be here. I'll be here as long as you're breathing!"

She didn't move. IV bag emptying, catheter bag filling.

Susan came in, her nurse's uniform rumpled. "Hi, Gene."

"Hello, Susan."

"We're about the same tonight."

I could see that. And then the Camineur kicked in and I could see something else, in one of those unbidden flashes of knowledge that Bucky called heightened connective cognition. Bucky hadn't phoned me because he didn't really want to know what had happened to those old people. He already had enough belief to satisfy himself. He just wanted J-24 cleared publicly, and he wanted me to start the stink that would do it. He was handing the responsibility for Rose Kaplan and Samuel Fetterolf and Lydia Smith and Giacomo della Francesca to me. Just the way he'd handed me the responsibility for his break with Father Healey the night of his attempted suicide. I'd been used.

"Fuck that!"

Susan turned, startled, from changing Margie's catheter bag. "I beg your pardon?"

Margie, of course, said nothing.

I limped out of the hospital room, ignoring the look on Susan's face. I was angrier than I had been in eighteen months. Anger pushed against the inside of my chest and shot like bullets through my veins.

Until the Camineur did its thing.

A dozen boys crowded the basketball hoop after school, even though it was drizzling. I limped toward my car. Just as I reached it, a red Mercedes pulled up beside me and Jeff Connors got out from the passenger side.

He wore a blue bandana on his head, and it bulged on the left side above the ear. Heavy bandaging underneath; somebody had worked on him. He also wore a necklace of heavy gold links, a beeper, and jacket of supple brown leather. He didn't even try to keep the leather out of the rain.

His eyes met mine, and something flickered behind them. The Mercedes drove off. Jeff started toward the kids at the hoops, who'd all stopped playing to watch the car. There was the usual high-fiving and competitive dissing, but I heard its guarded quality, and I saw something was about to go down.

Nothing to do with me. I unlocked my car door.

Jenny Kelly came hurrying across the court, through the drizzle. Her eyes flashed. "Jeff! Jeff!"

She didn't even know enough not to confront him in front of his customers. He stared at her, impassive, no sign of his usual likable hustle. To him, she might as well have been a cop.

"Jeff, could I see you for a minute?"

Not a facial twitch. But something moved behind his eyes.

"Please? It's about your little brother."

She was giving him an out: family emergency. He didn't take it.

"I'm busy."

Ms. Kelly nodded. "Okay. Tomorrow, then?"

"I'm busy."

"Then I'll catch you later." She'd learned not to argue. But I saw her face after she turned from the boys sniggering behind her. She wasn't giving up, either. Not on Jeff.

Me, she never glanced at.

I got into my car and drove off, knowing better than Jenny Kelly what was happening on the basketball court behind me, not even trying to interfere. If it didn't happen on school property, it would happen off it. What was the difference, really? You couldn't stop it. No matter what idealistic fools like Jenny Kelly thought.

Her earrings were little pearls, and her shirt, damp from the rain, clung to her body.

The whole next week, I left the phone off the hook. I dropped Libby a note saying to write me instead of calling because NYNEX was having trouble with the line into my building. I didn't go to the hospital. I taught my math classes, corrected papers in my own classroom, and left right after eighth period. I only glimpsed Jenny Kelly once, at a bus stop a few blocks from the school building. She was holding the hand of a small black kid, three or four, dressed in a Knicks sweatshirt. They were waiting for a bus. I drove on by.

But you can't really escape.

I spotted the guy when I came out of the metroteller late Friday afternoon. I'd noticed him earlier, when I dropped off a suit at the drycleaner's. This wasn't the kind of thing I dealt with anymore—but it happens. Somebody you collared eight years ago gets out and decides to get even. Or somebody spots you by accident and suddenly remembers some old score on behalf of his cousin, or your partner, or some damn thing you yourself don't even recall. It happens.

I couldn't move fast, not with my knee. I strolled into Mulcahy's, which has a long aisle running between the bar and the tables, with another door to the alley that's usually left open if the weather's any good. The men's and ladies' rooms are off an alcove just before the alley, along with a pay phone and cigarette machine. I nodded at Brian Mulcahy behind the bar, limped through, and went into the ladies'. It was empty. I kept the door cracked. My tail checked the alley, then strode toward the men's room. When his back was to the ladies' and his hand on the heavy door, I grabbed him.

He wasn't as tall or heavy as I was—average build, brown hair, nondescript looks. He twisted in my grasp, and I felt the bulge of the gun under his jacket. "Stop it, Shaunessy! NYPD!"

I let him go. He fished out his shield, looking at me hard. Then he said, "Not here. This is an informant hangout— didn't you *know*? Meet me at 248 West Seventieth, apartment 8. Christ, why don't you fix your goddamn *phone*?" Then he was gone.

I had a beer at the bar while I thought it over. Then I went home. When the buzzer rang an hour and a half later, I didn't answer. Whoever stood downstairs buzzed for ten minutes straight before giving up.

That night I dreamed someone was trying to kill Margie, stalking her through the Times Square sleaze and firing tiny chemically poisoned darts. I couldn't be sure, dreams being what they are, but I think the stalker was me.

The Saturday mail came around three-thirty. It brought a flat manilla package, no return address, no note. It was a copy of the crime-scene report on the deaths of Lydia Smith and Giacomo della Francesca.

Seven years as partners doesn't just wash away. No matter what the official line has to be.

There were three eight-by-ten color crime scene photos: an empty rooftop; Mrs. Smith's body smashed on the pavement below; della Francesca's body lying on the floor beside a neatly made bed. His face was in partial shadow but his skinny spotted hands were clear, both clutching the hilt of the knife buried in his chest. There wasn't much blood. That doesn't happen until somebody pulls the knife out.

The written reports didn't say anything that wasn't in the photos.

I resealed the package and locked it in my file cabinet. Johnny had come through; Bucky had screwed me. The deaths were suicides, just like Kelvin Pharmaceuticals said, just like the Department said. Bucky's superconnective pill was the downer to end all downers, and he knew it, and he was hoping against hope it wasn't so.

Because he and Tommy had taken it together.

I've moved, Bucky had said in his one message since he told me about J-24. I'd assumed he meant that he'd changed apartments, or lovers, or lives, as he'd once changed from fanatic seminarian to fanatic chemist. But that's not what he meant. He meant he'd made his move with J-24, because he wanted the effect for himself and Tommy, and he refused to believe the risk applied to him. Just like all the dumb crack users I spent sixteen years arresting.

I dialed his number. After four rings, the answering machine picked up. I hung up, walked from the living room to the bedroom, pounded my fists on the wall a couple times, walked back and dialed again. When the machine picked up I said, "Bucky. This is Gene. Call me *now*. I mean it—I have to know you're all right."

I hesitated…he hadn't contacted me in weeks. What could I use as leverage?

"If you don't call me tonight, Saturday, by nine, I'll…" What? Not go look for him. Not again, not like thirteen years ago, rushing out in pants and pajama top, Margie calling after me *Gene! Gene! For God's sake…*

I couldn't do it again.

"If you don't phone by nine o'clock, I'll call the feds with what I've found about J-24, without checking it out with you first. So *call me*, Bucky."

Usually on Saturday afternoon I went to the hospital to see Margie. Not today. I sat at my kitchen table with algebra tests from 7B spread over the tiny surface, and it took me an hour to get through three papers. I kept staring at the undecorated wall, seeing Bucky there. Seeing the photos of Lydia Smith and Giacomo della Francesca. Seeing that night thirteen years ago when Bucky had his stomach pumped. Then I'd wrench myself back to the test papers and correct another problem. *If train A leaves point X traveling at a steady fifty miles per hour at six A.M....*

If a bullet leaves a gun traveling at 1500 feet per second, it can tear off a human head. Nobody realizes that but people who have seen it. Soldiers. Doctors. Cops.

After a while, I realized I was staring at the wall again, and picked up another paper. *If 3X equals 2Y...* Some of the names on the papers I didn't even recognize. Who was James Dillard? Was he the tall quiet kid in the last row, or the short one in shoes held together with tape, who fell asleep most mornings? They were just names.

On the wall, I saw Jenny Kelly holding the hand of Jeff Connors's little brother.

At seven-thirty I shoved the papers into my briefcase and grabbed my jacket. Before I left, I tried Bucky's number once more. No answer. I turned off the living room light and limped along the hall to the door. Before I opened it, my foot struck something. Without even thinking about it, I flattened against the wall and reached behind me for the foyer light.

It was only another package. A padded mailer, nine by twelve, the cheap kind that leaks oily black stuffing all over you if you open it wrong. The stuffing was already coming out a little tear in one corner. There were no stamps, no address; it had been shoved under the door. Whoever had left it had gotten into the building—not hard to do on a Saturday, with people coming and going, just wait until someone else has unlocked the door and smile at them as you go in, any set of keys visible in your hand. In the upper left corner of the envelope was an NYPD evidence sticker.

I picked up the package just as the phone rang.

"Bucky! Where are—"

"Gene, this is Jenny Kelly. Listen, I need your help. Please! I just got a call from Jeff Connors, he didn't know who else to call…the police have got him barricaded in a drug house, they're yelling at him to come out and he's got Darryl with him, that's his little brother, and he's terrified—Jeff is—that they'll knock down the door and go in shooting…God, Gene, please go! It's only four blocks from you, that's why I called, and you know how these things work…please!"

She had to pause for breath. I said tonelessly, "What's the address?"

She told me. I slammed the receiver down in the midst of her thank-you's. If she'd been in the room with me, I think I could have hit her.

I limped the four blocks north, forcing my damaged knee, and three blocks were gone before I realized I still had the padded envelope in my hand. I folded it in half and shoved it in my jacket pocket.

The address wasn't hard to find. Two cars blocked the street, lights whirling, and I could hear more sirens in the distance. The scene was all fucked up. A woman of twenty-one or twenty-two was screaming hysterically and jumping up and down: "He's got my baby! He's got a gun up there! He's going to kill my son!" while a uniform who looked about nineteen was trying ineptly to calm her down. Her clothes were torn and bloody. She smacked the rookie across the arm and his partner moved in to restrain her, while another cop with a bullhorn shouted up at the building. Neighbors poured out onto the street. The one uniform left was trying to do crowd control, funneling them away from the building, and nobody was going. He looked no older than the guy holding the woman, as if he'd had about six hours total time on the street.

I had my dummy shield. We'd all had our shields duplicated, one thirty-second of an inch smaller than the real shield, so we could leave the real one home and not risk a fine and all the paperwork if it got lost. When I retired, I turned in my shield but kept the dummy. I flashed it now at the rookie struggling with the hysterical girl. That might cost me a lot of trouble later, but I'd worry about that when the time came.

The street thinking comes back so fast.

"This doesn't look right," I shouted at the rookie over the shrieking woman. She was still flailing in his hold, screaming, "He's got my baby! He's got a gun! For Chrissake, get my baby before he kills him!" The guy with the bullhorn stopped shouting and came over to us.

"Who are you?"

"He's from Hostage and Barricade," the rookie gasped, although I hadn't said so. I didn't contradict him. He was trying so hard to be gentle with the screaming woman that she was twisting like a dervish while he struggled to cuff her.

"Look," I said, "she's not the mother of that child up there. He's the perp's little brother, and she sure the hell doesn't look old enough to be the older kid's mother!"

"How do you—" the uniform began, but the girl let out a shriek that could have leveled buildings, jerked one hand free and clawed at my face.

I ducked fast enough that she missed my eyes, but her nails tore a long jagged line down my cheek. The rookie stopped being gentle and cuffed her so hard she staggered. The sleeve of her sweater rode up when he jerked her arms behind her back, and I saw the needle tracks.

Shit, shit, shit.

Two back-up cars screamed up. An older cop in plain clothes got out, and I slipped my dummy shield back in my pocket.

"Listen, officer, I *know* that kid up there, the one with the baby. I'm his teacher. He's in the eighth grade. His name is

Jeff Connors, the child with him is his little brother Darryl, and this woman is *not* their mother. Something's going down here, but it's not what she says."

He looked at me hard. "How'd you get that wound?"

"She clawed him," the rookie said. "He's from—"

"He phoned me," I said urgently, holding him with my eyes. "He's scared stiff. He'll come out with no problems if you let him, and leave Darryl there."

"You're his teacher? That why he called you? You got ID?"

I showed him my United Federation of Teachers card, driver's license, Benjamin Franklin Junior High pass. The uniforms had all been pressed into crowd control by a sergeant who looked like he knew what he was doing.

"Where'd he get the gun? He belong to a gang?"

I said, "I don't know. But he might."

"How do you know there's nobody else up there with him?"

"He didn't say so on the phone. But I don't know for sure."

"What's the phone number up there?"

"I don't know. He didn't give it to me."

"Is he on anything?"

"I don't know. I would guess no."

He stood there, weighing it a moment. Then he picked up the bullhorn, motioned to his men to get into position. His voice was suddenly calm, even gentle. "Connors! Look, we know you're with your little brother, and we don't want either of you to get hurt. Leave Darryl there and come down by yourself. Leave the gun and just come on down. You do that and everything'll be fine."

"He's going to kill my—" the woman shrieked, before someone shoved her into a car and slammed the door.

"Come on, Jeff, we can do this nice and easy, no problems for anybody."

I put my hand to my cheek. It came away bloody.

The negotiator's voice grew even calmer, even more reasonable.

"I know Darryl's probably scared, but he doesn't have to be, just come on down and we can get him home where he belongs. Then you and I can talk about what's best for your little brother...."

Jeff came out. He slipped out of the building, hands on his head, going, "Don't shoot me, please don't shoot me, don't shoot me," and he wasn't the hustler of the eighth grade who knew all the moves, wasn't the dealer in big gold on the basketball court. He was a terrified thirteen-year-old in a dirty blue bandana, who'd been set up.

Cops in body armor rushed forward and grabbed him. More cops started into the building. A taxi pulled up and Jenny Kelly jumped out, dressed in a low-cut black satin blouse and black velvet skirt.

"Jeff! Are you all right?"

Jeff looked at her, and I think if they'd been alone, he might have started to cry. "Darryl's up there alone...."

"They'll bring Darryl down safe," I said.

"I'll take Darryl to your aunt's again," Jenny promised. A man climbed out of the taxi behind her and paid the driver. He was scowling. The rookie glanced down the front of Jenny's blouse.

Jeff was cuffed and put into a car. Jenny turned to me. "Oh, your face, you're hurt! Where will they take Jeff, Gene? Will you go, too? Please?"

"I'll have to. I told them it was me that Jeff phoned."

She smiled. I'd never seen her smile like that before, at least not at me. I kept my eyes raised to her face, and my own face blank. "Who set him up, Jenny?"

"Set him up?"

"That woman was yelling she's Darryl's mother and Jeff was going to kill her baby. Somebody wanted the cops to go storming in there and start shooting. If Jeff got killed, the

NYPD would be used as executioners. If he didn't, he'd still be so scared they'll own him. Who is it, Jenny? The same one who circulated that inflammatory crap about a Neighborhood Safety Information Network?"

She frowned. "I don't know. But Jeff has been…there were some connections that…" She trailed off, frowned again. Her date came up to us, still scowling. "Gene, this is Paul Snyder. Paul, Gene Shaunessy…. Paul, I'm sorry, I have to go with Gene to wherever they're taking Jeff. I'm the one he really called. And I said I'd take Darryl to his aunt."

"Jenny, for Chrissake…we have tickets for the Met!"

She just looked at him, and I saw that Paul Snyder wasn't going to be seeing any more of Jenny Kelly's cleavage.

"I'll drive you to the precinct, Jenny," I said. "Only I have to be the first one interviewed, I have to be as quick as I can because there's something else urgent tonight…." Bucky. Dear God.

Jenny said quickly, "Your wife? Is she worse?"

"She'll never be worse. Or better," I said before I knew I was going to say anything, and immediately regretted it.

"Gene…" Jenny began, but I didn't let her finish. She was standing too close to me. I could smell her perfume. A fold of her black velvet skirt blew against my leg.

I said harshly, "You won't last at school another six months if you take it all this hard. You'll burn out. You'll leave."

Her gaze didn't waver. "Oh no, I won't. And don't talk to me in that tone of voice."

"Six months," I said, and turned away. A cop came out of the building carrying a wailing Darryl. And the lieutenant came over to me, wanting to know whatever it was I thought I knew about Jeff Connors's connections.

It was midnight before I got home. After the precinct house there'd been a clinic, with the claw marks on my face disinfected and a tetanus shot and a blood test and photographs for the assault charges. After that, I looked for Bucky.

He wasn't at his apartment, or at his mother's apartment. The weekend security guard at Kelvin Pharmaceuticals said he'd been on duty since four P.M. and Dr. Romano hadn't signed in to his lab. That was the entire list of places I knew to look. Bucky's current life was unknown to me. I didn't even know Tommy's last name.

I dragged myself through my apartment, pulling off my jacket. The light on the answering machine blinked.

My mind—or the Camineur—made some connections. Even before I pressed the MESSAGE button, I think I knew.

"Gene, this is Tom Fletcher. You don't know me...we've never met...." A deeper voice than I'd expected but ragged, spiky. "I got your message on Vince Romano's machine. About the J-24. Vince..." The voice caught, went on. "Vince is in the hospital. I'm calling from there. St. Clare's, it's on Ninth at Fifty-first. Third floor. Just before he...said to tell you..."

I couldn't make out the words in the rest of the message.

I sat there in the dark for a few minutes. Then I pulled my jacket back on and caught a cab to St. Clare's. I didn't think I could drive.

The desk attendant waved me through. He thought I was just visiting Margie, even at this hour. It had happened before. But not lately.

Bucky lay on the bed, a sheet pulled up to his chin but not yet over his face. His eyes were open. Suddenly I didn't want to know what the sheet was covering—how he'd done it, what route he'd chosen, how long it had taken. All the dreary algebra of death. *If train A leaves the station at a steady fifty miles per hour....* There were no marks on Bucky's face. He was smiling.

And then I saw he was still breathing. Bucky, the ever inept, had failed a second time.

Tommy stood in a corner, as if he couldn't get it together enough to sit down. Tall and handsome, he had dark well-cut hair and the kind of fresh complexion that comes with youth and exercise. He looked about fifteen years younger than Bucky. When had they taken the J-24 together? Lydia Smith and Giacomo della Francesca had killed themselves within hours of each other. So had Rose Kaplan and Samuel Fetterolf. How much did Tommy know?

He held out his hand. His voice was husky. "You're Gene."

"I'm Gene."

"Tom Fletcher. Vince and I are—"

"I know," I said, and stared down at Bucky's smiling face, and wondered how I was going to tell this boy that he, too, was about to try to kill himself for chemically induced love.

I flashed on Bucky and me sitting beside the rain-streaked alley window of the Greek diner. *What are you waiting for, Bucky, your prince to come?*

Yes. And, *Have you ever thought what it would be like to be really merged—to know him, to be him?*

"Tom," I said. "There's something we have to discuss."

"Discuss?" His voice had grown even huskier.

"About Bucky. Vince. You and Vince."

"What?"

I looked down at Bucky's smiling face.

"Not here. Come with me to the waiting room."

It was deserted at that hour, a forlorn alcove of scratched furniture, discarded magazines, too-harsh fluorescent lights. We sat facing each other on red plastic chairs.

I said abruptly, "Do you know what J-24 is?"

His eyes grew wary. "Yes."

"What is it?" I couldn't find the right tone. I was grilling him as if he were under arrest and I were still a cop.

"It's a drug that Vince's company was working on. To make people bond to each other, merge together in perfect union." His voice was bitter.

"What else did he tell you?"

"Not much. What should he have told me?"

You never see enough, not even in the streets, to really prepare you. Each time you see genuine cruelty, it's like the first time. Damn you, Bucky. Damn you to hell for emotional greed.

I said, "He didn't tell you that the clinical subjects who took J-24…the people who bonded…he didn't tell you they were all elderly?"

"No," Tom said.

"The same elderly who have been committing suicide all over the city? The ones in the papers?"

"Oh, my God."

He got up and walked the length of the waiting room, maybe four good steps. Then back. His handsome face was gray as ash. "They killed themselves after taking J-24? Because of J-24?"

I nodded. Tom didn't move. A long minute passed, and then he said softly, "My poor Vince."

"Poor *Vince*? How the hell can you…don't you get it, Tommy boy? You're next! You took the bonding drag with poor suffering Vince, and your three weeks or whatever of joy are up and you're dead, kid! The chemicals will do their thing in your brain, super withdrawal, and you'll kill yourself just like Bucky! Only you'll probably be better at it and actually succeed!"

He stared at me. And then he said, "Vince didn't try to kill himself."

I couldn't speak.

"He didn't attempt suicide. Is that what you thought? No, he's in a catatonic state. And *I* never took J-24 with him."

"Then who…"

"God," Tom said, and the full force of bitterness was back. "He took it with God. At some church, Our Lady of Everlasting Something. Alone in front of the altar, fasting and praying. He told me when he moved out."

When he moved out. Because it wasn't Tommy that Bucky really wanted, it was God. It had always been God, for thirteen solid years. *Tell Father Healey I can't touch God anymore....Have you ever thought what it would be like to be really merged, to know him to be him?*...No. To know Him. To be Him. *What are you waiting for, your Prince?*

Yes.

Tom said, "After he took the damned drug, he lost all interest in me. In everything. He didn't go to work, just sat in the corner smiling and laughing and crying. He was like... high on something, but not really. I don't know what he was. It wasn't like anything I ever saw before."

Nor anybody else. Merged with God. *They knew each other, they almost were each other. Think, Gene! To have an end to the terrible isolation in which we live our whole tiny lives....*

"I got so *angry* with him," Tom said, "and it did no good at all. I just didn't count anymore. So I told him to get out, and he did, and then I spent three days looking for him but I couldn't find him anywhere, and I was frantic. Finally he called me, this afternoon. He was crying. But again it was like I wasn't even really there, not me, Tom. He sure the hell wasn't crying over *me.*"

Tom walked to the one small window, which was barred. Back turned to me, he spoke over his shoulder. Carefully, trying to get it word-perfect.

"Vince said I should call you. He said, 'Tell Gene—it wears off. And then the grief and loss and anger...*especially* the anger that it's over. But I can beat it. It's different for me. They couldn't.' Then he hung up. Not a word to me."

I said, "I'm sorry."

He turned. "Yeah, well, that was Vince, wasn't it? *He* always came first with himself."

No, I could have said. God came first. And that's how Bucky beat the J-24 withdrawal. Human bonds, whether forged by living or chemicals got torn down as much as built up. But you don't have to live in a three-room apartment with God, fight about money with God, listen to God snore and fart and say things so stupid you can't believe they're coming out of the mouth of your beloved, watch God be selfish or petty or cruel. God was *bigger* than all that, at least in Bucky's mind, was so big that He filled everything. And this time when God retreated from him, when the J-24 wore off and Bucky could feel the bonding slipping away, Bucky slipped along after it. Deeper into his own mind, where all love exists anyway.

"The doctor said he might never come out of the catatonia," Tom said. He was starting to get angry now, the anger of self-preservation. "Or he might. Either way, I don't think I'll be waiting around for him. He's treated me too badly."

Not a long-term kind of guy, Tommy. I said, "But you never took J-24 yourself."

"No," Tom said. "I'm not *stupid*. I think I'll go home now. Thanks for coming, Gene. Good to meet you."

"You, too," I said, knowing neither of us meant it.

"Oh, and Vince said one more thing. He said to tell you it was, too, murder. Does that make sense?"

"Yes," I said. But not, I hoped, to him.

After Tom left, I sat in the waiting room and pulled from my jacket the second package. The NYPD evidence sticker had torn when I'd jammed the padded mailer in my pocket.

It was the original crime scene report for Lydia Smith and Giacomo della Francesca, the one Johnny Fermato must have known about when he sent me the phony one. This report was signed Bruce Campinella. I didn't know him, but I could probably pick him out of a line-up from the brief tussle in Mulcahy's: average height, brown hair, undistinguished looks, furious underneath. Your basic competent honest cop, still outraged at what the system had for sale. And for sale at a probably not very high price. Not in New York.

There were only two photos this time. One I'd already seen: Mrs. Smith's smashed body on the pavement below the nursing home roof. The other was new. Della Francesca's body lying on the roof, not in his room, before the cover-up team moved him and took the second set of pictures. The old man lay face up, the knife still in his chest. It was a good photo; the facial expression was very clear. The pain was there, of course, but you could see the fury, too. The incredible rage. *And then the grief and loss and anger… especially the anger that it's over.*

Had della Francesca pushed Lydia Smith first, after that shattering quarrel that came from losing their special, unearthly union, and then killed himself? Or had she found the strength in her disappointment and outrage to drive the knife in, and then she jumped? Ordinarily, the loss of love doesn't mean hate. Just how unbearable was it to have had a true, perfect, unhuman end to human isolation—and then *lose* it? How much rage did that primordial loss release?

Or maybe Bucky was wrong, and it had been suicide after all. Not the anger uppermost, but the grief. Maybe the rage on della Francesca's dead face wasn't at his lost perfect love, but at his own emptiness once it was gone. He'd felt something so wonderful, so sublime, that everything *else* afterward fell unbearably short, and life itself wasn't worth the effort. No matter what he did, he'd never ever have its like again.

I thought of Samuel Fetterolf before he took J-24, writing everyone in his family all the time, trying to stay connected. Of Pete, straining every cell of his damaged brain to protect the memories of the old people who'd been kind to him. Of Jeff Connors, hanging onto Darryl even while he moved into the world of red Mercedes and big deals. Of Jenny Kelly, sacrificing her dates and her sleep and her private life in her frantic effort to connect to the students, who she undoubtedly thought of as "her kids." Of Bucky.

The elevator to the fifth floor was out of order. I took the stairs. The shift nurse barely nodded at me. It wasn't Susan. In Margie's room the lights had been dimmed and she lay in the gloom like a curved dry husk, covered with a light sheet. I pulled the chair closer to her bed and stared at her.

And for maybe the first time since her accident, I remembered.

Roll the window down, Gene.

It's fifteen degrees out there, Margie!

It's real air. Chilled like good beer. It smells like a goddamn factory in this car.

Don't start again. I'm warning you.

Are you so afraid the job won't kill you that you want the cigarettes to do it?

Stop trying to control me.

Maybe you should do better at controlling yourself.

The night I'd found Bucky at Our Lady of Perpetual Sorrows, I'd been in control. It was Bucky who hadn't. I'd crawled back in bed and put my arms around Margie and vowed never to see Bucky and his messy stupid dramas of faith ever again. Margie hadn't been asleep. She'd been crying. I'd had enough hysteria for one night; I didn't want to hear it. I wouldn't even let her speak. I stalked out of the bedroom and spent the night on the sofa. It was three days before I'd even talk to her so we could work it out and make it good between us again.

Have a great year! she'd said my first September at Benjamin Franklin. But it hadn't been a great year. I was trying to learn how to be a teacher, and trying to forget how to be a cop, and I didn't have much time left over for her. We'd fought about that, and then I'd stayed away from home more and more to get away from the fighting, and by the time I returned *she* was staying away from home a lot. Over time it got better again, but I don't know where she was going the night she crossed Lexington with a bag of groceries in front of that '93 Lincoln. I don't know who the groceries were for. She never bought porterhouse and champagne for *me*.

Maybe we would have worked that out, too. Somehow.

Weren't there moments, Gene, Bucky had said, *when you felt so close to Margie it was like you crawled inside her skin for a minute? Like you* were *Margie?* No. I was never Margie. We were close, but not that close. What we'd had was good, but not *that* good. Not a perfect merging of souls.

Which was the reason I could survive its loss.

I stood up slowly, favoring my knee. On the way out of the room, I took the plastic bottle of Camineur out of my pocket and tossed it in the waste basket. Then I left, without looking back.

Outside, on Ninth Avenue, a patrol car suddenly switched on its lights and took off. Some kids who should have been at home swaggered past, heading downtown. I looked for a pay phone. By now, Jenny Kelly would be done delivering Darryl to his aunt, and Jeff Connors was going to need better than the usual overworked public defender. I knew a guy at Legal Aid, a hotshot, who still owed me a long-overdue favor.

I found the phone, and the connection went through.

THE MOUNTAIN TO MOHAMMED

> "*A person gives money to the physician.*
> *Maybe he will be healed.*
> *Maybe he will not be healed.*"
> —The Talmud

WHEN THE SECURITY BUZZER SOUNDED, Dr. Jesse Randall was playing *go* against his computer. Haruo Kaneko, his roommate at Downstate Medical, had taught him the game. So far nineteen shiny black and white stones lay on the grid under the scanner field. Jesse frowned; the computer had a clear shot at surrounding an empty space in two moves, and he couldn't see how to stop it. The buzzer made him jump.

Anne? But she was on duty at the hospital until one. Or maybe he remembered her rotation wrong...

Eagerly he crossed the small living room to the security screen. It wasn't Anne. Three stories below a man stood on the street, staring into the monitor. He was slight and fair, dressed in jeans and frayed jacket with a knit cap pulled low on his head. The bottoms of his ears were red with cold.

"Yes?" Jesse said.

"Dr. Randall?" The voice was low and rough.

"Yes."

92

"Could you come down here a minute to talk to me?"

"About what?"

"Something that needs talkin' about. It's personal. Mike sent me."

A thrill ran through Jesse. This was it, then. He kept his voice neutral. "I'll be right down."

He turned off the monitor system, removed the memory disk, and carried it into the bedroom, where he passed it several times over a magnet. In a gym bag he packed his medical equipment: antiseptics, antibiotics, sutures, clamps, syringes, electromed scanner, as much equipment as would fit. Once, shoving it all in, he laughed. He dressed in a warm pea coat bought second-hand at the Army-Navy store and put the gun, also bought second-hand, in the coat pocket. Although of course the other man would be carrying. But Jesse liked the feel of it, a slightly heavy drag on his right side. He replaced the disk in the security system and locked the door. The computer was still pretending to consider its move for *go*, although of course it had near-instantaneous decision capacity.

"Where to?"

The slight man didn't answer. He strode purposefully away from the building, and Jesse realized he shouldn't have said anything. He followed the man down the street, carrying the gym bag in his left hand.

Fog had drifted in from the harbor. Boston smelled wet and grey, of rotting piers and dead fish and garbage. Even here, in the Morningside Security Enclave, where that part of the apartment maintenance fees left over from security went to keep the streets clean. Yellow lights gleamed through the gloom, stacked twelve stories high but crammed close together; even insurables couldn't afford to heat much space.

Where they were going there wouldn't be any heat at all.

Jesse followed the slight man down the subway steps. The guy paid for both of them, a piece of quixotic dignity that made Jesse smile. Under the lights he got a better look: The man was older than he'd thought, with webbed lines around the eyes and long, thin lips over very bad teeth. Probably hadn't ever had dental coverage in his life. What had been in his genescan? God, what a system.

"What do I call you?" he said as they waited on the platform. He kept his voice low, just in case.

"Kenny."

"All right, Kenny," Jesse said, and smiled. Kenny didn't smile back. Jesse told himself it was ridiculous to feel hurt; this wasn't a social visit. He stared at the tracks until the subway came.

At this hour the only other riders were three hard-looking men, two black and one white, and an even harder-looking Hispanic girl in a low-cut red dress. After a minute Jesse realized she was under the control of one of the black men sitting at the other end of the car. Jesse was careful not to look at her again. He couldn't help being curious, though. She looked healthy. All four of them looked healthy, as did Kenny, except for his teeth. Maybe none of them were uninsurable; maybe they just couldn't find a job. Or didn't want one. It wasn't his place to judge.

That was the whole point of doing this, wasn't it?

The other two times had gone as easy as Mike said they would. A deltoid suture on a young girl wounded in a knife fight, and burn treatment for a baby scalded by a pot of boiling water knocked off a stove. Both times the families had been so grateful, so respectful. They knew the risk Jesse was taking. After he'd treated the baby and left antibiotics and analgesics on the pathetic excuse for a kitchen counter, a board laid across the non-functional radiator, the young Hispanic mother had grabbed his hand and covered it with kisses. Embarrassed, he'd turned to smile at her husband, wanting to say something, wanting to make clear he wasn't just another sporadic do-gooder who happened to have a medical degree.

"I think the system stinks. The insurance companies should never have been allowed to deny health coverage on the basis of genescans for potential disease, and employers should never have been allowed to keep costs down by health-based hiring. If this were a civilized country, we'd have national health care by now!"

The Hispanic had stared back at him, blank-faced.

"Some of us are trying to do better," Jesse said.

It was the same thing Mike—Dr. Michael Cassidy— had said to Jesse and Anne at the end of a long drunken evening celebrating the halfway point in all their residencies. Although, in retrospect, it seemed to Jesse that Mike hadn't drunk very much. Nor had he actually said very much outright. It was all implication, probing masked as casual philosophy. But Anne had understood, and refused instantly. "God, Mike, you could be dismissed from the hospital! The regulations forbid residents from exposing the hospital to the threat of an uninsured malpractice suit. There's no money."

Mike had smiled and twirled his glass between fingers as long as a pianist's. "Doctors are free to treat whomever they wish, at their own risk, even uninsurables. *Carter v. Sunderland*."

"Not while a hospital is paying their malpractice insurance as residents, if the hospital exercises its right to so forbid. *Janisson v. Lechchevko*."

Mike laughed easily. "Then forget it, both of you. It's just conversation."

Anne said, "But do you personally risk—"

"It's not right," Jesse cut in—couldn't she see that Mike wouldn't want to incriminate himself on a thing like this?— "that so much of the population can't get insurance. Every year they add more genescan pre-tendency barriers, and the poor slobs haven't even got the diseases yet!"

His voice had risen. Anne glanced nervously around the bar. Her profile was lovely, a serene curving line that reminded Jesse of those Korean screens in the expensive shops on Commonwealth Avenue. And she had lovely legs, lovely breasts, lovely everything. Maybe, he'd thought, now that they were neighbors in the Morningside Enclave...

"Another round," Mike had answered.

Unlike the father of the burned baby, who never had answered Jesse at all. To cover his slight embarrassment—the mother had been so effusive—Jesse gazed around the cramped apartment. On the wall were photographs in cheap plastic frames of people with masses of black hair, all lying in bed. Jesse had read about this: It was a sort of mute, powerless protest. The subjects had all been photographed on their death beds. One of them was a beautiful girl, her eyes closed and her hand flung lightly over her head, as if asleep. The Hispanic followed Jesse's gaze and lowered his eyes.

"Nice," Jesse said. "Good photos. I didn't know you people were so good with a camera."

Still nothing.

Later, it occurred to Jesse that maybe the guy hadn't understood English.

The subway stopped with a long screech of equipment too old, too poorly maintained. There was no money. Boston, like the rest of the country, was broke. For a second Jesse thought the brakes weren't going to catch at all and his heart skipped, but Kenny showed no emotion and so Jesse tried not to, either. The car finally stopped. Kenny rose and Jesse followed him.

They were somewhere in Dorchester. Three men walked quickly toward them and Jesse's right hand crept toward his pocket. "This him?" one said to Kenny.

"Yeah," Kenny said. "Dr. Randall," and Jesse relaxed.

It made sense, really. Two men walking through this neighborhood probably wasn't a good idea. Five was better. Mike's organization must know what it was doing.

The men walked quickly. The neighborhood was better than Jesse had imagined: small row houses, every third or fourth one with a bit of frozen lawn in the front. A few even had flower boxes. But the windows were all barred, and over all hung the grey fog, the dank cold, the pervasive smell of garbage.

The house they entered had no flower box. The steel front door, triple-locked, opened directly into a living room furnished with a sagging sofa, a TV, and an ancient daybed whose foamcast headboard flaked like dandruff. On the daybed lay a child, her eyes bright with fever.

Sofa, TV, headboard vanished. Jesse felt his professional self take over, a sensation as clean and fresh as plunging into cool water. He knelt by the bed and smiled. The girl, who looked about nine or ten, didn't smile back. She had a long, sallow, sullen face, but the long brown hair on the pillow was beautiful: clean, lustrous, and well-tended.

"It's her belly," said one of the men who had met them at the subway. Jesse glanced up at the note in his voice, and realized that he must be the child's father. The man's hand trembled as he pulled the sheet from the girl's lower body. Her abdomen was swollen and tender.

"How long has she been this way?"

"Since yesterday," Kenny said, when the father didn't answer.

"Nausea? Vomiting?"

"Yeah. She can't keep nothing down."

Jesse's hands palpated gently. The girl screamed.

Appendicitis. He just hoped to hell peritonitis hadn't set in. He didn't want to deal with peritonitis.

"Bring in all the lamps you have, with the brightest-watt bulbs. Boil water—" He looked up. The room was very cold. "Does the stove work?"

The father nodded. He looked pale. Jesse smiled and said, "I don't think it's anything we can't cure, with a little luck here." The man didn't answer.

Jesse opened his bag, his mind racing. Laser knife, sterile clamps, scaramine—he could do it even without nursing assistance provided there was no peritonitis. But only if… The girl moaned and turned her face away. There were tears in her eyes. Jesse looked at the man with the same long, sallow face and brown hair. "You her father?"

The man nodded.

"I need to see her genescan."

The man clenched both fists at his side. Oh, God, if he didn't *have* the official printout…Sometimes, Jesse had read, uninsurables burned them. One woman, furious at the paper that would forever keep her out of the middle class, had mailed hers, smeared with feces, and packaged with a plasticene explosive, to the President. There had been headlines, columns, petitions…and nothing had changed. A country fighting for its very economic survival didn't hesitate to expend front-line troops. If there was no genescan for this child, Jesse couldn't use scaramine, that miracle immune-system booster, to which about 15 percent of the population had a fatal reaction. Without scaramine, under these operating conditions, the chances of post-operation infection were considerably higher. If she couldn't take scaramine…

The father handed Jesse the laminated printout, with the deeply embossed seal in the upper corner. Jesse scanned it quickly. The necessary RB antioncogene on the eleventh chromosome was present. The girl was not potentially allergic to scaramine. Her name was Rosamund.

"Okay, Rose," Jesse said gently. "I'm going to help you. In just a little while you're going to feel so much better…"

He slipped the needle with anesthetic into her arm. She jumped and screamed, but within a minute she was out.

Jesse stripped away the bedclothes, despite the cold, and told the men how to boil them. He spread betadine over her distended abdomen and poised the laser knife to cut.

The hallmark of his parents' life had been caution. *Don't fall, now! Drive carefully! Don't talk to strangers!* Born during the Depression—the other one—they invested only in Treasury bonds and their own one-sixth acre of suburban real estate. When the marching in Selma and Washington had turned to killing in Detroit and Kent State, they shook their heads sagely: *See? We said so. No good comes of getting involved in things that don't concern you.* Jesse's father had held the same job for thirty years; his mother considered it immoral to buy anything not on sale. They waited until she was over 40 to have Jesse, their only child.

At 16, Jesse had despised them; at 24, pitied them; at 28, his present age, loved them with a despairing gratitude not completely free of contempt. They had missed so much, dared so little. They lived now in Florida, retired and happy and smug. "The pension"—they called it that, as if it were a famous diamond or a well-loved estate—was inflated by Collapse prices into providing a one-bedroom bungalow with beige carpets and a pool. In the pool's placid, artificially blue waters, the Randalls beheld chlorined visions of triumph. "Even after we retired," Jesse's mother told him proudly, "we didn't have to go backwards."

"That's what comes from thrift, son," his father always added. "And hard work. No reason these deadbeats today couldn't do the same thing."

Jesse looked around their tiny yard at the plastic ducks lined up like headstones, the fanatically trimmed hedge, the blue-and-white striped awning, and his arms made curious beating motions, as if they were lashed to his side. "Nice, Mom. Nice."

"You know it," she said, and winked roguishly. Jesse had looked away before she could see his embarrassment. Boston had loomed large in his mind, compelling and vivid and hectic as an exotic disease.

There was no peritonitis. Jesse sliced free the spoiled bit of tissue that had been Rosamund's appendix. As he closed with quick, sure movements, he heard a click. A camera. He couldn't look away, but out of a sudden rush of euphoria he said to whoever was taking the picture, "Not one for the gallery this time. This one's going to *live*."

When the incision was closed, Jesse administered a massive dose of scaramine. Carefully he instructed Kenny and the girl's father about the medication, the little girl's diet, the procedures to maintain asepsis which, since they were bound to be inadequate, made the scaramine so necessary. "I'm on duty the next thirty-six hours at the hospital. I'll return Wednesday night, you'll either have to come get me or give me the address, I'll take a taxi and—"

The father drew in a quick, shaky breath like a sob. Jesse turned to him. "She's got a strong fighting chance, this procedure isn't—" A woman exploded from a back room, shrieking.

"No, no, noooooo…" She tried to throw herself on the patient. Jesse lunged for her, but Kenny was quicker. He grabbed her around the waist, pinning her arms to her sides. She fought him, wailing and screaming, as he dragged her back through the door. "Murderer, baby killer, nooooooo—"

"My wife," the father finally said. "She doesn't…doesn't understand."

Probably doctors were devils to her, Jesse thought. Gods who denied people the healing they could have offered.

Poor bastards. He felt a surge of quiet pride that he could teach them different.

The father went on looking at Rosamund, now sleeping peacefully. Jesse couldn't see the other man's eyes.

Back home at the apartment, he popped open a beer. He felt fine. Was it too late to call Anne? It was—the computer clock said 2:00 A.M. She'd already be sacked out. In seven more hours his own 36-hour rotation started, but he couldn't sleep.

He sat down at the computer. The machine hadn't moved to surround his empty square after all. It must have something else in mind. Smiling, sipping at his beer, Jesse sat down to match wits with the Korean computer in the ancient Japanese game in the waning Boston night.

Two days later, he went back to check on Rosamund. The row house was deserted, boards nailed diagonally across the window. Jesse's heart began to pound. He was afraid to ask information of the neighbors; men in dark clothes kept going in and out of the house next door, their eyes cold. Jesse went back to the hospital and waited. He couldn't think what else to do.

Four rotations later the deputy sheriff waited for him outside the building, unable to pass the security monitors until Jesse came home.

COMMONWEALTH OF MASSACHUSETTS
SUFFOLK COUNTY SUPERIOR COURT

To _Jesse Robert Randall_ of _Morningside Security Enclave, Building 16, Apartment 3C, Boston_, within our county of Suffolk. Whereas _Steven & Rose Gocek_ of Boston within our County of Suffolk has begun an action of Tort against you returnable in the Superior Court holden at Boston within our County of Suffolk on _October 18,_

<u>2004 </u>, in which action damages are claimed in the sum of <u>$2,000,000 </u>—as follows:

TORT AND/OR CONTRACT FOR MALPRACTICE

as will more fully appear from the declaration to be filed in said Court when and if said action is entered therein:

WE COMMAND YOU, if you intend to make any defense of said action, that on said date or within such further time as the law allows you cause your written appearance to be entered and your written answer or other lawful pleadings to be filed in the office of the Clerk of the Court to which said writ is returnable, and that you defend against said action according to law.

Hereof fail not at your peril, as otherwise said judgment may be entered against you in said action without further notice.

Witness, <u>Lawrence F. Monastersky, Esquire </u>, at <u> Boston</u>, the <u> fourth </u> day of <u> March </u> in the year of our Lord two thousand <u> four </u>.

Alice P. McCarren
Clerk

Jesse looked up from the paper. The deputy sheriff, a soft-bodied man with small, light eyes, looked steadily back.

"But what…what happened?"

The deputy looked out over Jesse's left shoulder, a gesture meaning he wasn't officially saying what he was saying. "The kid died. The one they say you treated."

"Died? Of what? But I went back…" He stopped, filled with sudden sickening uncertainty about how much he was admitting.

The deputy went on staring over his shoulder. "You want my advice, doc? Get yourself a lawyer."

Doctor, lawyer, Indian chief, Jesse thought suddenly, inanely. The inanity somehow brought it all home. He was being sued. For malpractice. By an uninsurable. Now. Here. Him, Jesse Randall. Who had been trying only to help.

"Cold for this time of year," the deputy remarked. "They're dying of cold and malnutrition down there, in Roxbury and Dorchester and Southie. Even the goddamn weather can't give us a break."

Jesse couldn't answer. A wind off the harbor fluttered the paper in his hand.

"These are the facts," the lawyer said. He looked tired, a small man in a dusty office lined with second-hand law books. "The hospital purchased malpractice coverage for its staff, including residents. In doing so, it entered into a contract with certain obligations and exclusions for each side. If a specific incident falls under these exclusions, the contract is not in force with regard to that incident. One such exclusion is that residents will not be covered if they treat uninsured persons unless such treatment occurs within the hospital setting or the resident has reasonable grounds to assume that such a person is insured. Those are not the circumstances you described to me."

"No," Jesse said. He had the sensation that the law books were falling off the top shelves, slowly but inexorably, like small green and brown glaciers. Outside, he had the same sensation about the tops of buildings.

"Therefore, you are not covered by any malpractice insurance. Another set of facts: Over the last five years jury decisions in malpractice cases have averaged 85 percent in favor of plaintiffs. Insurance companies and legislatures are made up of insurables, Dr. Randall. However, juries are still drawn by lot from the general citizenry. Most of the educated general citizenry finds ways to get out of jury duty. They always did. Juries are likely to be 65 percent or more uninsurables.

It's the last place the have-nots still wield much real power, and they use it."

"You're saying I'm dead," Jesse said numbly. "They'll find me guilty."

The little lawyer looked pained. "Not 'dead,' Doctor. Convicted—most probably. But conviction isn't death. Not even professional death. The hospital may or may not dismiss you—they have that right—but you can still finish your training elsewhere. And malpractice suits, however they go, are not of themselves grounds for denial of a medical license. You can still be a doctor."

"Treating who?" Jesse cried. He threw up his hands. The books fell slightly faster. "If I'm convicted I'll have to declare bankruptcy—there's no way I could pay a jury settlement like that! And even if I found another residency at some third-rate hospital in Podunk, no decent practitioner would ever accept me as a partner. I'd have to practice alone, without money to set up more than a hole-in-the-corner office among God-knows-*who*…and even that's assuming I can find a hospital that will let me finish. All because I wanted to help people who are getting shit on!"

The lawyer took off his glasses and rubbed the lenses thoughtfully with a tissue. "Maybe," he said, "they're shitting back."

"What?"

"You haven't asked about the specific charges, Doctor."

"Malpractice! The brat died!"

The lawyer said, "Of massive scaramine allergic reaction."

The anger leeched out of Jesse. He went very quiet.

"She was allergic to scaramine," the lawyer said. "You failed to ascertain that. A basic medical question."

"I—" The words wouldn't come out. He saw again the laminated genescan chart, the detailed analysis of chromosome 11. A camera clicking, recording that he was there. The hysterical woman, the mother, exploding from the back room: *nooooooooooo…*The father standing frozen, his eyes downcast.

It wasn't possible.

Nobody would kill their own child. Not to discredit one of the fortunate ones, the haves, the insurables, the employables…No one would do that.

The lawyer was watching him carefully, glasses in hand.

Jesse said, "Dr. Michael Cassidy—" and stopped.

"Dr. Cassidy what?" the lawyer said.

But all Jesse could see, suddenly, was the row of plastic ducks in his parents' Florida yard, lined up as precisely as headstones, garish hideous yellow as they marched undeviatingly wherever it was they were going.

"No," Mike Cassidy said. "I didn't send him."

They stood in the hospital parking lot. Snow blew from the east. Cassidy wrapped both arms around himself and rocked back and forth. "He didn't come from us."

"He said he did!"

"I know. But he didn't. His group must have heard we were helping illegally, gotten your name from somebody—"

"But why?" Jesse shouted. "Why frame me? Why kill a child just to frame *me*? I'm nothing!"

Cassidy's face spasmed. Jesse saw that his horror at Jesse's position was real, his sympathy genuine, and both useless. There was nothing Cassidy could do.

"I don't know," Cassidy whispered. And then, "Are you going to name me at your malpractice trial?"

Jesse turned away without answering, into the wind.

Chief of Surgery Jonathan Eberhart called him into his office just before Jesse started his rotation. Before, not after. That was enough to tell him everything. He was getting very good at discovering the whole from a single clue.

"Sit down, Doctor," Eberhart said. His voice, normally austere, held unwilling compassion. Jesse heard it, and forced himself not to shudder.

"I'll stand."

"This is very difficult," Eberhart said, "but I think you already see our position. It's not one any of us would have chosen, but it's what we have. This hospital operates at a staggering deficit. Most patients cannot begin to cover the costs of modern technological health care. State and federal governments are both strapped with enormous debt. Without insurance companies and the private philanthropical support of a few rich families, we would not be able to open our doors to anyone at all. If we lose our insurance rating we—"

"I'm out on my ass," Jesse said. "Right?"

Eberhart looked out the window. It was snowing. Once Jesse, driving through Oceanview Security Enclave to pick up a date, had seen Eberhart building a snowman with two small children, probably his grandchildren. Even rolling lopsided globes of cold, Eberhart had had dignity.

"Yes, Doctor. I'm sorry. As I understand it, the facts of your case are not in legal dispute. Your residency here is terminated."

"Thank you," Jesse said, an odd formality suddenly replacing his crudeness. "For everything."

Eberhart neither answered nor turned around. His shoulders, framed in the grey window, slumped forward. He might, Jesse thought, have had a sudden advanced case of osteoporosis. For which, of course, he would be fully insured.

He packed the computer last, fitting each piece carefully into its original packing. Maybe that would raise the price that Second Thoughts was willing to give him: *Look, almost new, still in the original box.* At the last minute he decided to keep the playing pieces for *go*, shoving them into the suitcase with his clothes and medical equipment. Only this suitcase would go with him.

When the packing was done, he walked up two flights and rang Anne's bell. Her rotation ended a half hour ago. Maybe she wouldn't be asleep yet.

She answered the door in a loose blue robe, toothbrush in hand. "Jesse, hi, I'm afraid I'm really beat—"

He no longer believed in indirection. "Would you have dinner with me tomorrow night?"

"Oh, I'm sorry, I can't," Anne said. She shifted her weight so one bare foot stood on top of the other, a gesture so childish it had to be embarrassment. Her toenails were shiny and smooth.

"After your next rotation?" Jesse said. He didn't smile.

"I don't know when I—"

"The one after that?"

Anne was silent. She looked down at her toothbrush. A thin pristine line of toothpaste snaked over the bristles.

"Okay," Jesse said, without expression. "I just wanted to be sure."

"Jesse—" Anne called after him, but he didn't turn around. He could already tell from her voice that she didn't really have anything more to say. If he had turned it would have been only for the sake of a last look at her toes, polished and shiny as *go* stones, and there really didn't seem to be any point in looking.

He moved into a cheap hotel on Boylston Street, into a room the size of a supply closet with triple locks on the door and bars on the window, where his money would go far. Every morning he took the subway to the Copley Square library, rented a computer cubicle, and wrote letters to hospitals across the country. He also answered classified ads in the *New England Journal of Medicine*, those that offered practice out-of-country where a license was not crucial, or low-paying medical research positions not too many people might want, or supervised assistantships. In the afternoons he walked the grubby streets of Dorchester, looking for Kenny. The lawyer representing Mr. and Mrs. Steven Gocek, parents of the dead Rosamund, would give him no addresses. Neither would his own lawyer, he of the collapsing books and desperate clientele, in whom Jesse had already lost all faith.

He never saw Kenny on the cold streets.

The last week of March, an unseasonable warm wind blew from the south, and kept up. Crocuses and daffodils pushed up between the sagging buildings. Children appeared, chasing each other across the garbage-laden streets, crying raucously. Rejections came from hospitals, employers. Jesse had still not told his parents what had happened. Twice in April he picked up a public phone, and twice he saw again the plastic ducks marching across the artificial lawn, and something inside him slammed shut so hard not even the phone number could escape.

One sunny day in May he walked in the Public Garden. The city still maintained it fairly well; foreign tourist traffic made it profitable. Jesse counted the number of well-dressed foreigners versus the number of ragged street Bostonians. The ratio equaled the survival rate for uninsured diabetics.

"Hey, mister, help me! Please!"

A terrified boy, ten or eleven, grabbed Jesse's hand and pointed. At the bottom of a grassy knoll an elderly man lay crumpled on the ground, his face twisted.

"My Grandpa! He just grabbed his chest and fell down! Do something! Please!"

Jesse could smell the boy's fear, a stink like rich loam. He walked over to the old man. Breathing stopped, no pulse, color still pink…

No.

This man was an uninsured. Like Kenny, like Steven Gocek. Like Rosamund.

"Grandpa!" the child wailed. "Grandpa!"

Jesse knelt. He started mouth-to-mouth. The old man smelled of sweat, of fish, of old flesh. No blood moved through the body. "Breathe, dammit, breathe," Jesse heard someone say, and then realized it was him. "*Breathe*, you old fart, you uninsured deadbeat, you stinking ingrate, breathe—"

The old man breathed.

He sent the boy for more adults. The child took off at a dead run, returning twenty minutes later with uncles, father, cousins, aunts, most of whom spoke some language Jesse couldn't identify. In that twenty minutes none of the well-dressed tourists in the Garden approached Jesse, standing guard beside the old man, who breathed carefully and moaned softly, stretched full-length on the grass. The tourists glanced at him and then away, their faces tightening.

The tribe of family carried the old man away on a homemade stretcher. Jesse put his hand on the arm of one of the young men. "Insurance? Hospital?"

The man spat onto the grass.

Jesse walked beside the stretcher, monitoring the old man until he was in his own bed. He told the child what to do for him, since no one else seemed to understand. Later that day he went back, carrying his medical bag, and gave them the last of his hospital supply of nitroglycerin. The oldest woman, who had been too busy issuing orders about the stretcher to pay Jesse any attention before, stopped dead and jabbered in her own tongue.

"You a doctor?" the child translated. The tip of his ear, Jesse noticed, was missing. Congenital? Accident? Ritual mutilation? The ear had healed clean.

"Yeah," Jesse said. "A doctor."

The old woman chattered some more and disappeared behind a door. Jesse gazed at the walls. There were no deathbed photos. As he was leaving, the woman returned with ten incredibly dirty dollar bills.

"Doctor," she said, her accent harsh, and when she smiled Jesse saw that all her top teeth and most of her bottom ones were missing, the gum swollen with what might have been early signs of scurvy.

"Doctor," she said again.

He moved out of the hotel just as the last of his money ran out. The old man's wife, Androula Malakassas, found him a room in somebody else's rambling, dilapidated boardinghouse. The house was noisy at all hours, but the room was clean and large. Androula's cousin brought home an old, multi-positional dentist chair, probably stolen, and Jesse used that for both examining and operating table. Medical substances—antibiotics, chemotherapy, IV drugs—which he had thought of as the hardest need to fill outside of controlled channels, turned out to be the easiest. On reflection, he realized this shouldn't have surprised him.

In July he delivered his first breech birth, a primipara whose labor was so long and painful and bloody he thought at one point he'd lose both mother and baby. He lost neither, although the new mother cursed him in Spanish and spit at him. She was too weak for the saliva to go far. Holding the warm-assed, nine-pound baby boy, Jesse had heard a camera click. He cursed too, but feebly; the sharp thrill of pleasure that pierced from throat to bowels was too strong.

In August he lost three patients in a row, all to conditions that would have needed elaborate, costly equipment and procedures: renal failure, aortic aneurysm, narcotic overdose. He went to all three funerals. At each one the family and friends cleared a little space for him, in which he stood surrounded by respect and resentment. When a knife fight broke out at the funeral of the aneurysm, the family hustled Jesse away from the danger, but not so far away that he couldn't treat the loser.

In September a Chinese family, recent immigrants, moved into Androula's sprawling boarding house. The woman wept all day. The man roamed Boston, looking for work. There was a grandfather who spoke a little English, having learned it in Peking during the brief period of American industrial expansion into the Pacific Rim before the Chinese government convulsed and the American economy collapsed. The grandfather played *go*. On evenings when no one wanted Jesse, he sat with Lin Shujen and moved the polished white and black stones over the grid, seeking to enclose empty spaces without losing any pieces. Mr. Lin took a long time to consider each move.

In October, a week before Jesse's trial, his mother died. Jesse's father sent him money to fly home for the funeral, the first money Jesse had accepted from his family since he'd finally told them he had left the hospital. After the funeral Jesse sat in the living room of his father's Florida house and listened to the elderly mourners recall their youths in the vanished prosperity of the 1950s and '60s.

"Plenty of jobs then for people who're willing to work."

"Still plenty of jobs. Just nobody's willing any more."

"Want everything handed to them. If you ask me, this collapse'll prove to be a good thing in the long run. Weed out the weaklings and the lazy."

"It was the sixties we got off on the wrong track, with Lyndon Johnson and all the welfare programs—"

They didn't look at Jesse. He had no idea what his father had said to them about him.

Back in Boston, stinking under Indian summer heat, people thronged his room. Fractures, cancers, allergies, pregnancies, punctures, deficiencies, imbalances. They were resentful that he'd gone away for five days. He should be here; they needed him. He was the doctor.

The first day of his trial, Jesse saw Kenny standing on the courthouse steps. Kenny wore a cheap blue suit with loafers and white socks. Jesse stood very still, then walked over to the other man. Kenny tensed.

"I'm not going to hit you," Jesse said.

Kenny watched him, chin lowered, slight body balanced on the balls of his feet. A fighter's stance.

"I want to ask something," Jesse said. "It won't affect the trial. I just want to know. Why'd you do it? Why did *they*? I know the little girl's true genescan showed 98% risk of leukemia death within three years, but even so—how could you?"

Kenny scrutinized him carefully. Jesse saw that Kenny thought Jesse might be wired. Even before Kenny answered, Jesse knew what he'd hear. "I don't know what you're talking about, man."

"You couldn't get inside the system. Any of you. So you brought me out. If Mohammed won't go to the mountain—"

"You don't make no sense," Kenny said.

"Was it worth it? To you? To them? Was it?"

Kenny walked away, up the courthouse steps. At the top waited the Goceks, who were suing Jesse for $2,000,000 he didn't have and wasn't insured for, and that they knew damn well they wouldn't collect. On the wall of their house, wherever it was, probably hung Rosamund's deathbed picture, a little girl with a plain, sallow face and beautiful hair.

Jesse saw his lawyer trudge up the courthouse steps, carrying his briefcase. Another lawyer, with an equally shabby briefcase, climbed in parallel several feet away. Between the two men the courthouse steps made a white empty space.

Jesse climbed, too, hoping to hell this wouldn't take too long. He had an infected compound femoral fracture, a birth with potential erythroblastosis fetalis, and an elderly phlebitis, all waiting. He was especially concerned about the infected fracture, which needed careful monitoring because the man's genescan showed a tendency toward weak T-cell production. The guy was a day laborer, foul-mouthed and ignorant and brave, with a wife and two kids. He'd broken his leg working illegal construction. Jesse was determined to give him at least a fighting chance.